17 Alma Road

Other Books by Ian Gouge

Novels and Novellas

Tilt - Coverstory books, 2023
Once Significant Others - Coverstory books, 2023
On Parliament Hill - Coverstory books, 2021
A Pattern of Sorts - Coverstory books, 2020
The Opposite of Remembering - Coverstory books, 2020
At Maunston Quay - Coverstory books, 2019
An Infinity of Mirrors - Coverstory books, 2018 (2nd ed.)
The Big Frog Theory - Coverstory books, 2018 (2nd ed.)
Losing Moby Dick and Other Stories - Coverstory books, 2017

Short Stories

An Irregular Piece of Sky - Coverstory books, 2023
Degrees of Separation - Coverstory books, 2018
Secrets & Wisdom - Paperback, 2017

Poetry

Grimsby Docks - Coverstory books, 2024
Crash - Coverstory books, 2023
not the Sonnets - Coverstory books, 2023
Selected Poems: 1976-2022 - Coverstory books, 2022
The Homelessness of a Child - Coverstory books, 2021
The Myths of Native Trees - Coverstory books, 2020
First-time Visions of Earth from Space - Coverstory books, 2019
After the Rehearsals - Coverstory books, 2018
Punctuations from History - Coverstory books, 2018
Human Archaeology - Paperback, 2017
Collected Poems (1979-2016) - KDP, 2017

Non-Fiction

Shrapnel from a Writing Life - Coverstory books, 2022

Ian Gouge

17 Alma Road

Coverstory books

First published in paperback and ebook
formats by Coverstory books, 2024

ISBN 978-1-7384693-83 (Paperback)
ISBN 978-1-7384693-90 (eBook)

www.iangouge.com

www.coverstorybooks.com

I

If he cannot recall where he spent the first four years of his life, he knows it might just as well have been 17 Alma Road. Indeed, in many respects that was where his and Maddie's lives actually started. As the two of them gradually matured their aunt and uncle attempted to furnish them with the components from which they could compile an adequate backstory. Owen had come to regard these individual narratives as fairy tales, as if Augustus and Alice had not been their parents but were figures as imaginary as Hansel and Gretel. Although he now can piece together the last five decades of the house before which he stands, Owen is also conscious of the gaps in the pre-history which had been imparted to the two of them, a piecemeal compendium of fragments which he knows on occasion choose to contradict each other. Had he been tempted to press Florence to fill in all the spaces he believed existed, the opportunity to do so was removed that Waitrose Thursday with the sudden collapse which saw her inadvertently propel her trolley into the side of a parked 'C'-class Mercedes. Thus it can only be shards of their shared history — his and Maddie's, Florence and George's, even Augustus and Alice's — which come back to him almost as pinpricks of light.

Where the long chain of iron spikes is cemented into the top of the wall, the metal — corroded by the onslaught of rain across the years — has bled onto the stone. It is an unequal and unhappy marriage of both form and colour, discordant in both senses. Allowing his fingers to worry at rust which looks almost volcanic in its eruption from the base of the points, he is surprised how easy it is to lift a little of the crusted iron here and there, thus restoring the slabs beneath to late autumn's afternoon light. And — as if that were not miracle enough — he is also struck by how pale the re-exposed stone is, and how the impersonating lava, focussed on its own incursion, has inadvertently shielded these small areas. Both invader and protector at the same time. How was that even possible?

Having been distracted, he now looks through the railing to the house beyond, his hand tracing a path down the block-work before instinctively finding its way to his trouser pocket, feeling for a key that used to be there. Wasn't that how his life had been, encapsulated right there in limestone and iron: the fusion of both pain and pleasure, risk and reward? Or all their lives — though in Maddie's case reward had proven hard to come by. However he might choose to categorise them, the blend of such experiences had been responsible for fashioning what he had become — even if he is, at this precise moment, unable to recognise in himself anything approaching the fabric of either iron or stone. Were he feeling fanciful, might he not consider himself an example of moderately successful fusion, the amalgam of opposing forces, evidence of a joint victory for metal and mineral? Or, if he felt in a blacker mood, the defeat of both.

And yet it is more than metaphor, this wall and the house beyond. The wall is a barrier, certainly; as much a barrier as the house had been. A construct designed to keep things in or out, separated from whatever might exist on the other side. Years later, standing here again, the wall still performs its function to perfection in spite of the compromised railings. There is a gate of course, the same gate he would have occasionally swung on as a child; but now it is evidently so rarely used that he suspects he would be unable to shift it with the same childhood ease. He glances along to the break in the wall, to the space which frames the gate, and wonders if it has been padlocked — and if not, whether he should try its latch one final time. No-one would stop him. After all, what would any passer-by see other than a late middle-aged man in decent enough shoes and a heavy coat; a man well enough dressed to pass as an estate agent, or perhaps someone with a legitimate interest in the house? Which without doubt he has.

Much like the iron railings atop the wall (which have not been treated or painted for some while) the garden has gone a little to ruin too. It is easy enough to make out its general layout: where shrubs delineated the path up to the front door, and where the space opened out to give way to lawn. But the buddleia and cornus have not been pruned for many months such that — along with patches where weeds and a few invasive species have taken over — the garden appears unkempt and unruly. He can still make out traces of the flagstone path of course, and the invasion has not been so comprehensive as to remove all evidence of the lawn; yet even so, he feels as if he is staring at loss or capitulation.

And the house itself? Apparently intact. The sash windows look sound and the front door is as dark and solid as he had always known it. The lime render has cracked a little here and there, and in some places it too has been usurped by nature, a combination of climbing hydrangea and darker ivy seemingly in a race to the gutter at the top of the house, a race he is confident the ivy will win. The overall effect is somewhat taking however, and he is sure that anyone who might glance over the wall would regard the general facade as charming — even if such a sentiment would immediately be chased away by regret that the house has fallen into neglect. Indeed, it is hard to escape the fact that the place is letting the street down somewhat, playing odd-one-out with an array of neatly clipped hedges, well-tended gardens. Against such a model of comfortable suburban existence, were such onlookers of an imaginative or speculative disposition they might also have attempted to sketch out a history for the place and wondered, given the nature of its surroundings, how the house had come to this — and then simply carried on walking, always supposing the house had been worthy of them breaking stride in the first place. The more commercially-minded might just have wondered what it was worth.

But he knows most of the house's recent history — it is as much his story as the house's after all — and so can chart the journey from how it had been when he had lived there to how it stands today. There are episodes which inevitably elude him, fragments where he lost touch with the house as much as he did its inhabitants, though not through disinterest but because he was out of the country, wrapped up in other houses, other gardens. And other victories and defeats? Inevitably.

And 'worth'; how might you quantify that? "Not everything can be easily measured in pounds, shillings and pence" his aunt had once said to him as they sat in front of the fire. Even now he can picture the scene, and vaguely recalls that at the time he had been young enough to qualify as a child yet old enough to be on the threshold of beginning to understand the value of money. And "pounds, shillings and pence"? That leant a date to the incident: before 1971. But only just. He turned six in 1971, almost simultaneously with the country's shift to decimalisation. For a while ten or fifteen years ago he had wondered if he might be witness to a second such migration — from the pound to the euro — but this never materialised, much to the chagrin of Maddie and the delight of his aunt.

Florence once described herself as 'an Empire girl', bound-up in the traditions of a Britain long since vanquished. If the general populous had been weaned off such notions during the latter part of the twentieth century, there were many things to which Florence seemed determined to cling. Wreckage or not, if the pound had fallen (and, as she saw it, "to the Germans, of all people!") then he sensed she might have sunk along with it — and what would *that* have said about the rest of them? The fact that she had managed to hold on for another few pragmatic years — until a massive stroke did for her that black Thursday just as she was wheeling her shopping out of Waitrose — demonstrated both longevity and perseverance. The sudden nature of her end led some at her funeral to confess themselves grateful — such a passing was "a blessing" — although one or two of her erstwhile friends were secretly glad to see the back of her.

Did he miss her? Even if it would have been an entirely redundant question, he had imagined Maddie asking "Do you miss her, Glen?" soon after Florence's death. Although christened Owen, Maddie had chosen to call him 'Glen' ever since a history lesson at school during which she had been introduced to the legendary Welsh soldier and nationalist, Owen Glendower. Not only were they not Welsh, the young Owen showed no indication that he would make either an effective soldier or nationalist. Maddie had simply liked the sound of the words together.

"Don't we all?" he might have replied, his answer to her question implicit in his own.

And does Owen still miss her now — Florence, that is — as he stands looking up at the first-floor windows: the one that had been his, Maddie's next to it, Florence's on the end?

She and George had been ensconced in that room when he and Maddie arrived bereft and unwanted in the summer of 1969, suddenly-orphaned children who, when faced with being thrown upon the mercy of Social Services' bureaucracy, found themselves rescued by their Aunt and Uncle. Alice, their mother, had been an only child, and Florence was their father Augustus' only sibling. Such dramatic consequences would have been far from the mind of the inebriated lorry driver who, on rounding a blind bend too much outside of his lane, met their parents' car head-on. It had been a moment of madness which had not only killed its occupants in a brutal collision, but unravelled all that had gone before as well as the future plans already laid out for all the members of the family. As a quartet they had more or less mapped out the next twenty years, all the way through to Maddie's graduation from a university somewhere unspecified, proudly following in her big brother's footsteps. Given they were just four and two respectively, he and Maddie had been too young to make any contribution to the conversations which led to such conclusions; but Augustus and Alice had been progressive enough to ensure that their children were at least in the same room in which the relevant conversations were taking place even if they could have no possible idea what was actually bring discussed. Perhaps it was not surprising that Florence and George were made of similar stuff, shared the same aspirations for their nephew and niece; so much so that in the end their parents' tragedy impinged on the children for less than a year — at least in a practical sense. It was, to be sure, a year of upheaval and trauma, trauma and upheaval, but once they had settled down — the four of them — a new kind of normality took over. As Florence and George became their de facto parents, memories of their real mother and father faded quickly. If Maddie chose on occasion to suggest she could still remember them, Owen let her indulge her fantasy. For his part, he recalled nothing.

All of which means there is no existing connection between the house before him now — Florence and George's house — with Augustus and Alice other than an increasingly remote familial tie. Although hardly possible in his parents' case, he has an inkling that the rest of them might have left a ghostly imprint somewhere about the place, a tangible spectre that —

if he chose — he could lift and examine as easily as he had raised those small chunks of rust from the limestone coping. And could he? Should he? Is that, after all, why he is standing here now, hand once again on the garden wall, his eyes scanning the scene almost as if he were looking for clues? Does Owen need the house to respond to his prompting? Or does it work the other way round, the house and garden as the catalyst for memory, precisely as that far bedroom window made him think of Florence in a concrete way — and for the first time in what seems a very long time?

Are any of those questions resolved before he reaches the front gate and leans against it just to see?

II

And, his foot against the bottom rail, move it does, though stiffly of course. He knows its resistance is due to rust on the hinges and the tufts of weed against which he has to push in order to get the gate open far enough for him to step through. Once across the boundary he can see that the path is reasonably intact, and so — brushing his way past an ancient hebe and a briar rose of some persuasion — he walks the few yards necessary to find himself standing once again before the front door. Though badly tarnished, the old chrome digits '1' and '7' are still there. He resists the urge to try and wipe them clean with his coat sleeve. Instead, he turns ninety degrees and walks along the left half of the front of the house and onto the lawn where, after another pace or two, he turns again this time to examine the easterly aspect. The side of the building is much like the front, the garden here similarly unruly; ahead of him the old hedge George used to tend so lovingly has lost all sharp definition. Perhaps it is this neglect which strikes Owen as the saddest of all. Part-way along the hedge, he can still make out the arch which leads through to the back garden, and, without any premeditation or conscious decision-making, he walks through the space, almost apologetically brushing the encroaching branches aside.

Akin to the front, the framework of the back garden remains intact, pretty much as he had always known it: the long herbaceous borders running down each side, the three apple trees two-thirds of the way back (and to which George used to refer as his 'orchard') and beyond that the small vegetable patch with the raised beds where Florence would try — and fail — to grow carrots and onions each year. All have surrendered to time: the borders are weed-filled; the apple trees vast and unruly; the vegetable patch virtually indistinguishable in a tangle of weed and long grass. Owen wonders when the lawn last saw a mower, and who had wielded it. As he scans, he sees the old uneven patio George had laid one summer to accompany a grand idea about 'al fresco eating', and there, at a jaunty angle between house and garden — as it always had been — the ornate iron bench Florence had bought on a whim that same year. It had been, she said "George's patio's christening present". They had all laughed.

It is a recollection which makes him smile; a smile which can only be enhanced by the sight of Maddie sitting there, looking his way. He lifts a hand in a shy half-wave, and finds himself walking towards her.

"I thought I might find you here," Owen says as he comes to a halt in front of her, turning again to take in the entirety of the garden before sitting down in the space she has left for him.

"Where else?"

"Indeed."

"It's a shame," she says.

"What is?"

"Uncle George's trees. How they've been neglected. I've never seen them in such a state."

There is something in her tone which suggests more than simple regret.

"You've been back before?"

She returns her gaze from the orchard.

"On and off." She pauses. "It's like a tangible way to watch time pass, seeing the garden grow then wither, season by season. It's mushy underneath the trees where early apples have fallen and not been harvested. Of course the birds have helped themselves, but there is far too much fruit."

"There always was even when we were kids." He wonders when much becomes too much.

"And about two months ago," she says, her tone that of someone answering a question. Seeing the look of puzzlement on Owen's face she clarifies: "When the lawn was last cut. You were wondering. It must have been someone the estate agent sent round - though as far as I can see that's been the extent of their recent devotion to the place."

He looks over his shoulder to where the house squats behind them as if eavesdropping on their conversation.

"I'm surprised they haven't been able to sell it."

"Are you?" The soft incredulity in her voice forces him to turn to her again. "Wasn't it just bad timing, Aunt dying when she did, and then to be followed by the pandemic, the lockdowns?

What chance did the house have?" She speaks of it as if it were a person, an old friend.

"I suppose you're right."

"So the mowing was probably an attempt to smarten the place up, the belated reward for coming out of lockdown."

"If so, it was never going to be enough." He surprises himself with how definitive he is. The lack of care and attention seems almost a betrayal, as he feels as if he is responding to that inadequacy on behalf of the house. They are silent for a moment.

"Not surprising, though."

"What's not surprising?"

"That it hasn't sold. Considering." She leaves the word hanging.

"Considering what? The price? I thought I'd set a fair one — though I'm not entirely sure how the market has moved in the last three years or so."

"Not the price. Rather how unloved it looks."

"It was never unloved."

She smiles at his leaping to the house's defence again.

"*We* loved it; of course we did. All four of us. But if we were coming to it cold, today, and without our history… Think about what you'd see, Glen: overgrown garden, render shot to pieces, ivy climbing up the walls. An outsider could only assume it was just as neglected on the inside. They wouldn't see it for the lovely house it is, but rather a major project, a money pit."

Unsuccessfully, he tries to fold himself into the ignorance of someone who hadn't grown up in the house, who hadn't lived there for the best part of twenty years; someone who — until relatively recently — had never failed to return year after year not only to see Florence and George, but to breathe the place in again.

"Which is why I wondered whether or not you were tempted?"

"Tempted?" He seeks clarification.

"To take it on. To give the old place a new lease of life."

Although Maddie makes her question sound naïve and innocent, from his perspective it is nothing of the sort. It is one he has asked himself on multiple occasions, always able to find reasons for not taking up the challenge. Usually he has attributed his lack of enthusiasm to inconvenience or negative economics, or because doing so was personally inconvenient, his work taking precedence. But he knows that last excuse is one which is no longer valid.

"I don't know," Owen says, vaguely. It feels like honesty. "I suppose I've always assumed that I'd had my chance. When the question arose — front and centre at the reading of Florence's will — I wasn't in a position to… " He is suddenly unsure how to finish that particular sentence. "I mean, I thought it wasn't practical; that I would be better off with the cash."

"Doesn't that seem a little — sacrilegious?"

"What?"

"Exchanging the house for money. Doesn't that devalue what it meant to us — to you — and everything it stood for?"

"You've always said as much."

"Have I?" She smiles as if amused at the thought of repeating herself. "And now?"

"Now what?"

"Why are you back? What brings you here? What has changed that makes things — different?"

"How do you know they're different?" He tries to sound defiant. Or innocent. Maddie laughs, and waits.

Standing, he takes one step away from the bench and pauses; then, sensing she is tagging along behind him, begins a slow circuit of the garden. To his left there is a confusion of straggly rose bushes and weeds, the tell-tale signs of ancient shrubs that have given up the fight.

"I've stopped my wanderings," is how he chooses to phrase it, a somewhat flowery term which elicits another brief laugh from Maddie.

"You sound as if you're trying to make redundancy sound romantic rather than commercial," she observes, "as if you always had a choice in the matter."

"Didn't I?"

"Not really."

"I could have given up, walked away whenever I wanted." He is conscious of the hollowness of his assertion. "It was only a job, after all."

"And one you loved. Or" — she senses he is about to interrupt — "a nomadic lifestyle you were addicted to: all planes, trains, and automobiles."

"Perhaps," he concedes. "But that's all over now. Finally. And for good." He realises he sounds relieved.

"For good?"

He nods. "Now there's a new question."

"About the house?"

"About what next." He stops by one of the apple trees and allows a hand to brush some of its already-turning leaves. "And where next. And landing on the what and the where will confirm that I need the money from the sale to make those things happen. All the while I was" — he searches for a word eventually settling on an inadequate one — "away, it didn't matter. It was effectively money in the bank. But now…"

"Isn't that the wrong way round?"

About to move on again, Maddie's question stops him.

"What do you mean?"

"The what and where. All that nonsense." There is a change of tone in her voice, a seriousness verging on the scolding. "Isn't the 'where' obvious? Isn't the 'where' here? Surely that's why you've come back, to affirm that?"

It is a notion he had played with right up until the moment he stood before the house and picked rust from the old railing. Contrary to what Maddie might have been thinking, he had come back to be certain that the 'where' was *not* here, not on Alma Road amid the security of this quiet middle-class street where as many trees as parked cars delineated the road. But now here was a contemporary version of Maddie throwing everything into confusion once again, that old magic trick of hers.

He turns to look at the house and wonders whether 'right' and 'wrong' apply in this instance; whether what happens next should be governed by heart or head. And he wonders too how much influence his sister still has over him after all this time — even under present circumstances. If she is right about the hold his job had over him for all those prior years, might she not be right about this too? How much free will does he actually have? How much did any of them have? Wanting to be certain of his own independence, Owen can't help but recall that Maddie was always the one who seemed most determined to prove that she could do whatever she wanted, and whenever she wanted to do it. Yet he also can't help but wonder whether she would have been so determined so had she known the price she would have to pay.

The house looks back at him, its windows like eyes, behind each one a panoply of stories available for playback as soon as he crosses the threshold. To trigger them, to resurrect them and make them instantly available, all he needs to do is call the estate agent and make a different set of plans.

"Wouldn't it be like coming home?" Maddie asks.

III

She always had faith in the house. Indeed, one of her defining characteristics had been how wholeheartedly she threw herself into things; not necessarily situations or anything concrete, but concepts with potentially nebulous but life-changing outcomes. Maddie was a person who 'believed'. There was nothing half-hearted about her attachments. As he sees her walking beside him now, Owen can do nothing other than regard their present interaction as a perfectly natural extension of their interlocking lives, Maddie's presence nothing less than proof of the veracity of her personal philosophy — and the fact that 17 Alma Road had been one of the few constant and reliable things in her turbulent and all too-short life. Not that forty-nine was short in comparison to many of course, but Maddie had always laid out goals for herself by the decade. To the detached observer these may well have appeared as frivolous and intangible aspirations, but for her they were the earnest and incontrovertible goals by which she navigated. Hers was a commitment which, on more than one occasion, had led her to taking a wrong turn.

"When I am fifty," she had said to him as they sat on the patio drinking wine, for once their independent returns to visit Florence and George coinciding, "I will start being brilliant." It had been eight years earlier.

He had laughed. "How so?"

"Because I will have made all my mistakes and learned all my lessons by then; the veil will have been lifted. I will be back on the straight-and-narrow. There will be no more secrets hidden from me."

"You believe that?"

"I do." She was definite. "Let's face it, my twenties and thirties weren't up to much — even if in one sense they were."

"Again, how so?"

"Because of what I learned in that time. And for the last few years I've been putting those lessons to good use, sorting stuff out, mustering my troops."

Although he might have chosen to challenge her assertion, circumstantial evidence suggesting otherwise, the vague military analogy made him laugh.

"What's so funny?" She was momentarily serious.

"You are." Owen swayed back on the seat as she feigned to hit him. "Your grand plans; always so certain."

"You can be what you want to be and when you want to be it — even if you choose not to see it that way, brother mine. Pick a future, settle on an ambition, make it happen. Why not? Who's to stop you, other than yourself?"

It was a conversation they'd had at regular intervals ever since her last year at University when, in response to his asking about what she was going to do next, she had laid out her 'life plan' for him. Revisiting that plan and taking soundings on progress was all part of their familial ritual — and a ritual almost always played out in Alma Road. It was safe and neutral territory, the heart of things, almost as if the house was a place where anything and everything became possible. More than once she defended her various transgressions, teased him that some of the machinations via which she steered her way through life were things only she could see: "you don't have the imagination for it" she'd said without malice, as if it were indisputable fact.

"So I have to wait another three years before I see my sister being brilliant?"

"You do." She ignored the playful tone in his voice.

"That's hardly fair."

"What's hardly fair?" Prompted by the sound of laughter coming to her through the open kitchen window, Florence had emerged from the house and now stood at Maddie's end of the bench, a quarter-full wine bottle in her hand. "I thought you might want to finish this off."

Owen stood to cede his space to his aunt, walking the few paces necessary to retrieve a wicker seat from under the lean-to near the back door then returning to place it on the grass in front of them both.

"So, what's hardly fair?" Florence held out the wine to Maddie as she repeated herself, the younger woman refilling her glass and then passing the bottle to Owen.

"That I have to wait for Maddie to be brilliant."

"Isn't she brilliant already?" It always amazed Owen that when Florence smiled the years seemed to slip from her face; she was suddenly in her early sixties rather than late seventies. It was a smile that sometimes took him all the way back to his childhood. "Hasn't she always been brilliant?"

"Sis?"

Maddie had laughed at his invitation to justify herself and instead taken a sip of wine.

"Where's uncle George?" She ducked Owen's question.

"Oh, asleep in his study as usual. One glass of wine of a Sunday lunch and the man's completely useless. I swear he's getting worse. When he should be out here tending the beds or mowing the lawn he can't help himself but retreat for a quiet snooze."

"Isn't he allowed?" Maddie asked.

"Only when he's earned it. And as I keep telling him, being eighty-three is an excuse for nothing. He always was inclined to malinger."

Owen laughed. This was a familiar vaudeville routine, George the butt of Florence's jokes, often in absentia. Even though he knew none of it was meant, there were times when Owen couldn't help but wonder whether there were truths beneath the surface — hidden from he and Maddie — which may have provided some justification for Florence's theatrical complaint.

What would brook no doubt was Florence's unswerving faith in Maddie. In his own case, his aunt had treated him as he assumed her generation always considered men: they were the practical ones whose purpose was to earn the income, fight wars when wars needed fighting and, yes, mow lawns when the grass needed to be cut. Although born in 1938, Owen knew her memories of the Blitz (she had lived in London then) would have been virtually non-existent, her assessment of the war — and the men who fought in it — garnered from propaganda and popular culture. She had once confessed to a soft spot for Jack Hawkins, old black-and-white war films, and Ealing comedies. Based on such a philosophy, as a reasonable intelligent and logical man Owen would always be fine; he would do what needed to be done. She carried none of the reservations in relation to his dedication to his work about which Maddie occasionally confessed disquiet. He was simply doing what men did; in a way he was following in George's footsteps, and if George had been good enough for her...

But Maddie was a different prospect altogether; she needed nurturing and encouraging. If Florence felt this was part of her mission, she did so in order that Maddie - like Owen - would turn out to be a prime specimen based upon her own templates for people. Perhaps this dedication was especially pertinent given the siblings had no-one else to whom they could reasonably turn. So, while Owen's course was set on the practical and pragmatic, Maddie was destined to be artistic and gently temperamental; where he was good with numbers and mechanical things, she would be the creative one. It was this commitment which saw Florence harvest much of Maddie's work during the two-and-a-half decades after she left university, hanging paintings first in the hall downstairs then up the stairs themselves and eventually beyond. And as if such a gallery were insufficient, the occasional small scale sculpture would find its way onto a bookshelf or mantlepiece.

"This house is like a private gallery," he whispered to Maddie one day when Florence was out of earshot.

"Or a shrine," Maddie suggested. She had been in her early thirties; a self-confessed 'difficult period'.

That Sunday afternoon when the wine was being finished off much was as it had always been. In the intervening years Maddie had begged one or two pieces back from Florence in exchange for new ones claiming she had someone who was 'interested'. From time-to-time there were sales, the odd contribution to a minor show. Through all of this, Maddie's commitment to her plan — her upcoming brilliance — remained resolute, even if as a person she began to grow increasingly fragile. And Florence? As if to compensate for Maddie's decline, her belief in her surrogate daughter increased in equal measure.

"What are you thinking about?"

Maddie's voice drags him forward and deposits him back by the apple trees looking up at the disconsolate house.

"Oh, nothing. Just the past."

"'The past is another country'; isn't that what they say?"

"Who?"

"No idea." He hears the tell-tale tick in her voice which always suggested to him the suppression of a giggle. "Maybe you should look it up."

He resumes his walk, circling the trees before heading back towards the house, examining the second border and trying to recall how resplendent it had been. And could be again; who was to say?

"Whatever happens," he jumps back into the contemporary conversation which inexplicably has the feel of one broken from an age ago, "there will be some things to be rescued."

"Rescued?"

"From storage. Florence had some lovely furniture, didn't she? There are some pieces I'd like to give a new home to."

"Or an old one…"

Owen ignores the comment, preferring to go on the offensive.

"I might even want to salvage some of those old daubings of yours."

"You always were an ignorant bastard," Maddie says, the joke bringing a new lightness to her voice.

"Or I could see if I could sell some. On eBay maybe. Might get a few quid; enough to buy a take-away."

"Oh, my treat!"

The exaggeration in her response makes him stop. For a moment he closes his eyes as if doing so will allow him to call her work to mind, to reimagine the parade of paintings that graced the stairs. Yet at that moment he can only recall the large abstract which had hung above the dining room fireplace.

"What is it?" he asked her once.

"Not telling," she had been a little belligerent that afternoon. "One day, when you're old enough and wise enough, you might understand."

He wondered if he might be wise enough now and, if so, how he would respond to seeing it again. It was contemplation accompanied by a query as to whether, if he did indeed try and rescue her paintings, the only way of truly doing so would be to re-hang them in the self-same locations. But that could only mean one thing. Looking back to the house, he imagines himself on its far side where the dining room window looked out onto a narrow strip of lawn and the large beech hedge which separated it from number nineteen. Everything was connected — the garden, the lawn, the bench, he, Maddie, George and Florence — and the spider at the centre of the web was the house itself, a large square Edwardian edifice into and around which they had all fitted. And, it seemed, continued to do so.

IV

They had responded to the news in the way they thought you were supposed to react to such things: a blend of surprise, seriousness, joy. Having seen some of their friends go through a similar process and exposing such emotions, they assumed there was a template to which they needed to conform and so strived to do so; it didn't seem to matter how accurate an assumption that might be — valid or otherwise — nor how closely they adhered to it. In any event, it was an excuse for the party at the start of which Alice set-out saying she had forsworn drink for the duration, yet later succumbed to finish the evening almost as inebriated as Augustus.

For anyone who knew them — "AA" as they had become jointly known (accompanied by unoriginal jokes relating to either driving or drinking) — the party ran pretty much to form: three hours in the pub followed by another couple back at their flat for selected invitees only. A triumph in terms of the expectations one might have for an AA 'bash', it was an event that could easily have been concocted to celebrate a birthday or a new job — apart from the plethora of mainly pink 'congratulations' cards (not that they gave the colour any real thought at the time). In this instance, several months later the pink was to prove inappropriate: Owen was very definitely not a girl. Two years later they went through the same palaver, more or less, though with most of its elements curtailed: they spent less time in the pub; Alice drank less; not quite so many people came back to the flat. And not only was there less pink (even if was to prove apposite this time) there were fewer cards altogether. Whilst not entirely subdued, Augustus chose to blame the lack of scale on the realities of being a parent. "Alice is pretty tired these days, and Owen's a handful."

In truth they were both drained, partly by the burden of having to look after an infant, and somewhat obtusely partly from the removal of many of the social stimulants with which — as a childless couple — they had become accustomed. If, in retrospect, that first mid-sixties party came to symbolise anything it was less the celebration of an impending child and more the death knell for the kind of life they had been living. No-one had told them that would happen; there was nothing in their fictional template to forecast such a decline; the pink congratulations-cards failed to mention it. They had seen the impact in others of course — the sudden lurch into domesticity — but assumed that somehow it would not apply to them. After all they were not "those kind of people".

What kind of people were Augustus and Alice? They already had a plan which both pre-dated and precluded children: a future mapped out not in the concrete but in the abstract; one more concerned with 'how' they would live their lives rather than the specific episodes from which it would be comprised. Thus when they went to Italy for a holiday the year after their marriage, the scenery and the fabric of the buildings mattered less than their interaction with them. Whether they were in Rome or Pisa or Siena was — on one level — an irrelevance; what mattered was how they engaged with those cities, the restaurants they patronised, the cafés outside which they sat in order to absorb them. They wanted to be subsumed and integrated, not float over the top. Tourists took photographs and moved on; what Augustus and Alice wanted was to take Italy home in their souls. Whether romantic or naïve — or indeed able to be described in any other language aside from Italian — they were disinclined to give this shared ambition a label; it was simply who they were, a predilection or instinct which formed part of the magnetism which bound them together. If, having spent far more than planned, they returned home poorer than expected and therefore needed to tighten the purse strings for a few weeks afterwards, they persuaded themselves it was a small inconvenience for being richer in spirit. And what was money for anyway if not that?

The first six months of parenthood had, in Augustus' own words, "been hell" — even if Alice was the one who suffered most. Owen had not been a great sleeper and suffered from regular bouts of colic. As a couple without ties or responsibilities, traditionally it had been during late nights and very early mornings when they had come into their own, 'the life and souls of the party'; but after the summer of sixty-six the darkest hours were transformed into minefields across which Owen innocently stretched the trip-wires that could send them spiralling out of control.

With free evenings to themselves a rarity, when one did come around Augustus and Alice threw themselves into it with gusto, tired or not. For a few short hours their flame burned as brightly as ever, and old friends — those devoid of the burdens of parenthood — welcomed their comrades back into the fold, only to watch them almost inexplicably collapse and bring the evening to a sudden end. For both Augustus and Alice such falls were further and the landings harder than any they had previously known; they were the harbingers of the next day's hangovers inevitably laced with additional pain. Returning home to relieve the babysitter, they were thrust back into a remorseless cycle dominated by Owen, the child oblivious to their drunkenness and headaches, their desire for nothing but sleep. When perpetually haggard friends told them "don't worry, it gets better" it was a promise they wanted to believe in, especially Alice who, unlike Augustus, did not have the escape of a day job into which she could retreat. Owen *was* her day job.

So when news of Madeleine's imminent arrival broke, there seemed less cause to celebrate than before. Whether planned or accidental neither of them admitted; rather they found themselves united by the horror of staring into the void of mid-night crying and gruesome nappies which now would last twice as long. If they felt tricked by life they never let on. To their credit, where such a prospect saw other couples buckle, it actually brought Augustus and Alice closer together; they became allies above all else, even if never openly admitting who their common enemies might be. Given their own parents were either dead or living too far away to be of any material use they 'dug in', hunkered down for the long haul. From the rubble of Owen's first two years they managed to fashion a new regime, one which seemed to work well-enough. As the lesser of all evils, in the main it was a spartan kind of existence, at least socially; one punctuated by the odd oasis of revelry — oases which required considerable forethought and planning in order to be savoured.

"You know," Augustus said one evening, the two of them collapsed into the living room sofa, "it's a good job I don't have a role like Jeff's: management responsibility, always on the road. He says he's hardly home."

"I thought that's what you were aspiring to, one day." Alice added the last two words almost as an afterthought, as if she were offering him a way out.

"It was." He paused. "I mean, it is. When the time's right. Perhaps in five or six years when the kids have started school and the burden has eased."

Although she said nothing, Alice wondered if the burden would ever ease. It might shift somehow, move to a different plain, take on an alternative guise, but it would always be there — as she must be, constantly at Owen and Maddie's beck and call. If there was a pecking order she knew she had slipped down it; that they both had. And she could pin point exactly when that had happened. When would it revert so that she could put herself back on the top step once again? That was an unspoken question to which none of her friends ever offered an answer. She imagined she knew, but it was too dark a space into which to stare.

"That would be good," she said to him, trying to be enthusiastic, to find a middle way, a little light in the gloom. "After all, they'll be galloping away then, growing fast, learning things, needing books. Everything will be more" — she search for a word, desperate to avoid the obvious — "sophisticated."

Augustus laughed and stroked her arm. He had already been passed over for promotion once, and he feared the same would happen at the next review cycle. There was only so long he could remain a live candidate. When he said "five or six years" he might just as well have said decades. Or millennia.

Trapped together in various ways, they sought individual means of solace, some form of life-raft which might keep them afloat until rescue came — whether that would be in five years or fifty. Augustus endeavoured to keep his efforts work-related in order to ensure he didn't impact on his time with Alice and the children. It would have been all too easy to seek out things to keep him away from home, and though he may have been tempted he resisted that particular call. If some were surprised, more praised his dedication. He couldn't help but think that those who kept their opinions to themselves might secretly be closer to understanding the truth of his situation. And so the things for which he volunteered were small scale low-grade projects, working parties, corporate initiatives. These were easy to justify both to Alice and — more importantly — to himself; they would keep him visible, 'on the radar'. Not a naturally ambitious or corporate individual, his motivations were entirely practical and pragmatic, the ultimate goal being a better paid and more flexible job which would allow him — allow the two of them — to one day resume something akin to their old life.

Without such a framework to build on, Alice's opportunities were limited both in terms of the time she had available and the circles in which she moved. She made an extra effort to befriend one or two of the other mums at the toddlers' group, and set aside two hours every Thursday afternoon when — indulging the expense of a baby sitter — she joined an art group at the local library. The latter was not because she had any natural talent, but because absorbing herself in drawing and painting meant she didn't have to think about either

Owen or Maddie — at least not until the end of class when she would leave to go home and thus resume the cycle again.

"That's really good," Augustus said one Thursday evening after the children had gone to bed, holding up the still life she had worked on earlier in the day.

"I'm not so sure," she said, "the vase is a little wonky I think, and the shadow on that bottle's not quite right." She wasn't fishing for compliments but rather revelling in the delight of having something talk about other than the children — that and the fact that the spotlight was on her.

"Really?" Although he could see what she meant, Augustus didn't let on. "That never stopped Picasso."

"Picasso!" She laughed and thumped him gently on the arm.

"How long are you going to carry on?"

"'Carry on'?" The phrase struck her as odd.

"At the art class. Or did you say there was a finite end? I forget."

"It runs through term-time; numbers drop off during the holidays. Then, as far as I understand it, it keeps regenerating term after term. So I thought I'd carry on going until I couldn't."

"What would stop you?"

She weighed the question carefully, knowing there were multiple ways it could be interpreted. There was no reason for Augustus to be anything other than genuinely interested, no ulterior motive in play, so she set the tone for her response accordingly.

"Until they throw me out for being rubbish." They both laughed. "Or until the logistics with Owen and Maddie make it impossible."

"How so?"

"Oh, I don't know. New schools, new timetables, a change in circumstances. You know."

And Augustus did know. If Alice had asked him a parallel question relating to how long he might continuing working where he currently was, his initial answer might have proven identical. After that? Until he'd had enough, or knew it was a dead-end? Or perhaps the two of them might wake up one day and find themselves inclined to move house, move town — and all for a change of scenery. Such an impulse carried the mystique and lure of potentially feeling like a triumph, a trophy salvaged from the cabinet of the past.

For the next couple of years that was how they muddled on, the profile of their lives defined by the demands made of them by Owen and new-born Maddie, timetables set according to a meta-language in which words such as 'sitter', 'holiday', 'drop-off' and 'pick-up' became the most crucial. The currency by which they had once lived their lives was lost to memory. In as much as they were cocooned in new words, old ones — such as 'carefree' — became as contemporary as the dinosaur. Occasionally there were brief moments of brilliance. Most often these highlights revolved around the four of them taking advantage of sunny weekends, but just occasionally they were the gift of larger gatherings. Owen's fourth birthday proved to be one such gem, panned from the sludge of everyday mundanity. Although neither of them said anything a the time, there was a moment part-way through his party — amid the general noise and chaos — when they exchanged smiles, each of them independently thinking that perhaps this specific experience offered an inkling, an insight into how things could be in future. Might it yet be that those people who had told them three years previously "it gets better" had known what they were talking about after all?

They were never to weigh the validity of those assertions.

Where Augustus worked, one of the highlights of the year was the Summer Ball, a tradition which receded into the past further than anyone could remember and which — for reasons of politics and morale — successive management teams had shied away from mothballing. Not only had 'The Ball' come to be invested with its own aura and mythology, it also helped define the company, set it apart from the competition. Or at least that's what the staff told themselves. "The opposition may have their fancy golf days," a manager once said to Augustus, "but we have 'The Ball'" — not that Augustus and Alice had been able to attend since Owen's birth. But now he was four and finally behaving himself, content to be left with a baby-sitter, and with Maddie finally settling into a reliable routine, the tide seemed to be turning.

"The Ball," Augustus said during a quiet moment in front of the television one evening.

"What about it?"

"They want to know if we're going."

Alice had straightened in her chair.

"Going?"

"Yes." He allowed the words to swim in her consciousness for a moment or two. "What do you think?"

"I don't know." She might as well have been asked if she fancied a quick trip to the moon and back.

"We could get Mia to sit for us; perhaps with her friend — Polly, isn't it? — for added security. A chance to have some time to ourselves. Some 'glam' time." It was a crude invitation, designed to appeal to Alice's feminine side: the opportunity to dress up; baubles, bangles and bright shiny beads.

"Do you think we could?"

Augustus, having already made up his own mind, could tell in the tone of her question Alice was four-square with him — all she needed was permission to feel as he did.

"It's been five years since we last went; don't you think we deserve a little time off for good behaviour? Haven't we earned it? We needn't be out too late; leave just after the speeches and before the dancing gets out of hand. Midnight. Maybe a little after."

Having been waiting for her at the foot of the stairs, when Alice appeared above him in her long navy blue gown and jewellery — full battle dress — Augustus was transported; not merely back to previous Balls, but to those very early days after he first met her, the first time they went anywhere 'proper' together, their first holiday. The wedding.

"Will I do?" she asked a little coquettishly, knowing full well the answer.

A lump stuck in his throat.

Other than those for whom it was their birthday or wedding day, for the general populous there was nothing remarkable or celebratory about the 21st June. Certainly not Barry Webster who, a little while after nine, left 'The Red Lion' just outside Melton Mowbray and climbed into the cab of his truck. His own battle dress was nothing more than a scruffy pair of jeans, a t-shirt, and a sweatshirt that had seen better days, the official branding of the product it promoted having changed twice since his garment had been new. Staying in the pub longer than he had intended at least gave him the advantage of knowing the motorway would be relatively quiet; it would take him just over thirty minutes to reach the M1, after which it was simple a matter of the long slog north. Around two hours. Boredom, not traffic, was his greatest enemy.

Driving was Barry's life. It was all he knew. It had cost him two marriages, and his health was beginning to suffer. Overweight and under-exercised, he cut the kind of figure which conformed to most people's image of a long-distance lorry driver — especially when slouched in burger outlets at motorway services killing time he didn't have. Not that Barry was a 'bad' man in any true sense of the word; it was rather that he was lost. Or perhaps he had never really found himself.

Pulling off the motorway a little after midnight and within twenty minutes of home — a somewhat dilapidated upper floor flat in a badly converted semi on the wrong side of town — he had allowed his mind to stray. Conscious of his stay in 'The Red Lion', he had driven all the way north with special care, but being just a few miles from his destination — and on a road he knew so well — he allowed his concentration to waiver for just a moment. It was the wrong time for both tiredness and the alcohol to hit him.

He said he didn't see the car coming towards him because of the bend. Claimed it was the other vehicle that had strayed outside of their lane. Then in desperation he suggested that the car he hit had not had its headlights on. But the scars on the road, the wreckage, and his breath-test soon revealed the truth. In court, before he was sentenced, he was asked what he remembered of the crash. All he could recall was sound.

There had been nothing visual about his coming together with the pale blue Escort. He had heard the screaming crunch of metal on metal; felt himself rise into the air as his cab gouged its way across the bonnet of the car. Then as he dropped back down — the cab coming to rest against a hedge in a small ditch by the side of the road — he heard nothing but a vague hissing emanating from his engine.

He scrambled out of his cab, saw what was left of the Escort, and threw up.

V

"What choice do we have?"

"Choice?" George looked at Florence, unsure if he had misheard her. With her meaning usually so easy to decipher through her tone of voice, he was momentarily confused by its flatness.

"Yes, choice. That Torrington woman says that unless we step into the breech they will be farmed out to some dreadful couple."

"Did she say that: 'farmed out'?"

Seeing her fuss with the kettle, George found more evidence that Florence's normally peerless equilibrium had been upset by the situation in which Owen and Madeleine now found themselves — never mind the impact of the death of their parents, her brother.

"Not exactly."

"Nor the notion of there being a 'dreadful couple' waiting to harvest them." His tone was out of kilter with the situation; it he couldn't help himself, it was soon evident that his attempt to help her relax via a little lightness had failed.

'No, George, not that either." Florence allowed the kettle to hit the worktop with an exaggerated bang. Then her tone softened as it edged closer to despair. "But you know what I mean."

She had moved into a kind of over-drive since the news of the crash had broken (a one a.m. call from the police), rousting George along to drive to Augustus and Alice's house to rescue their nephew and niece. Chastising herself for the noise she had just made, Florence looked up to the ceiling as if it might be possible to see through the plaster, joists and carpet, and into the room where the two children had eventually settled back to sleep. She had tried to make light of their late night rescue from the baby-sitter, suggesting that a visit to their aunt and uncle's had been part of Mummy and Daddy's plans all along. Although the children had been tired, it had proved a ruse which generated sufficient excitement for it to be carried off. If the truth had to be broken in some way shape or form later that day it was a prospect to which neither of them was looking forward.

"I do."

"So why did you say 'choice' like that?"

"Like what?"

"I don't know. As if you didn't recognise that there was one to be made. Or as if having any kind of say in the matter was out of the question."

"And isn't it?"

"George, will you stop asking me questions back and give me a straight answer!" Florence couldn't help but give vent to her frustration. It was a modest explosion but nothing more than that, over in a moment.

George smiled a little sadly. He was used to Florence's questions being rhetorical, and had assumed 'what choice do we have' had fallen into that category.

"Of course it's out of the question that we should even consider sacrificing them to some unknown 'dreadful couple' — unless that dreadful couple happens to be us."

He did not mean to play with her in any way, but he'd become the kind of man whose natural instinct was to display his emotions subtly. Thus his anger was always modest, his enthusiasm tempered, his agreement never appearing entirely wholehearted. Just at that moment he was full-square behind his wife even if — in her unnatural state of agitation — she couldn't quite see it.

"And it should be us, shouldn't it?" Florence didn't wait for a response perhaps fearing another question from him. "What other outcome is acceptable for the children?"

"There is none," he offered, almost as if it were an effort to be quite that categorical. "Choice doesn't really come into it."

Florence walked across the kitchen to the table and sat down next to him. Somewhere about her she felt a weight shift, though she was unsure whether it was one being lifted from her or loaded upon her shoulders.

"But you can't have had much of a chat with that woman?"

"Torrington?" She paused, grateful that he was moving them along. "Not really. Enough to assure her that we were a safe haven for a short while, if only to prevent them from being carted off."

"And after that?"

"Those were almost my exact words: 'and after that?'" Florence paused to place her hand on the teapot then allowed it to remain there. "We only had a few minutes out of earshot of the children while you were helping them to pack the things they needed. She said there would be a file opened; that in the normal course of events — if there were no relatives close enough — they would be looked after by some temporary carers."

"'Close enough'?"

"I think she meant geographically. Or maybe familial. In any event at some point they would be 'processed', which, she said, might take a while given they're so young. Apparently older children are harder to place but easier to move around, though I'm not sure how that works. Perhaps they're more adaptable, I don't know. But she did suggest we could apply if we wanted to."

In a gesture unmissable by his wife, George shook his head.

"Makes them sound like a commodity; something to be traded."

"She'll be here tomorrow morning, around ten."

As if the prospect of the forthcoming visit was some kind of bookend, Florence sighed and rose, taking the teapot to the kettle where she freshened it with hot water. Doing so represented a lull, giving both of them a chance to regroup, to muster their thoughts accordingly, knowing what must come next.

George was ready for her when she returned with the pot to the table. "Do you think we qualify?"

She poured tea into their cups while she stood, and then resumed both her seat and her train of thought.

"There's a lot in our favour. We're family. We know the children — and the children know us. We're solvent. Given I'm only just Augustus' senior, I assume we're not too old." Though there was a slight quiver in her voice at this, she pushed on. "And we're stable. All that sort of stuff must count for something. And I suppose from her perspective — Torrington's, I mean — we'd be an easy option."

"For her, you mean?"

"I suppose so. And for the children too."

There was one last question to ask. They both knew it — and George knew he needed to be the one to do so.

"I think that's one of the reasons she's coming round," Florence continued, as if to put off the moment she knew was coming. "She'll want to see the children here, look over the house, get a sense of the place, the environment."

"And us too." It was almost a question, but not quite. Certainly not the other one George had on the tip of his tongue.

"Yes."

Florence allowed a gap to build, created a space in the conversation akin to opening a door and inviting George to walk through. He did so obligingly — and because he had no alternative.

"And what about us, Flo?"

"Us?"

Now it was her turn to seek clarification — even if she knew exactly what he meant. Was it that he had already expanded the word 'us' to mean the four of them rather than simply she and him? Because in many ways that was what she sought: not only to know who he was talking about but how his mind was working; to understand if he had already moved on.

"Not having children. Or not being able to have any." George was worried about his phrasing, how he was supposed to encapsulate in words what they had already experienced in an alternative context. Determined to avoid any sense of bad luck or fate's cruelty — and of apportioning blame — he had tried to hit the right note, neither resentful nor resigned, neither defeated nor victorious. Not being able to have children of their own had been a topic which had consumed them several years previously, a difficult period of upset and uncertainty — particularly for Florence, he thought — when emotions had fluctuated, sometimes wildly. Now suddenly there they were, and although admittedly not their own, two children *were* asleep just a few feet above them and innocently heralding the prospect of a changed future ahead. Certainly their presence would represent a divergence from the future they had planned, or had been forced to plan. 'Choice' was therefore about so much more than protecting Owen and Madeleine.

"I know," Florence said. "I know."

George waited a little more, for the phrase that surely must follow: her own redefinition of 'us', if that was indeed what she intended to do. Yet he wasn't sure.

"You know I was always keen. Before, I mean. And so…" Unsure how he should go on, he left the phrase there for her.

"I know," she said for the third time, though without any immediate follow-up, almost as if she had been sitting there alone and engaged in the process of convincing herself of something. Florence was well aware of what George was expecting to hear but instead chose a different tack. "And back then we changed our plans accordingly, didn't we? An alternative plan based on the fact that it would be just the two of us forever: what we would do, where we would live, where to take our holidays… An agenda for our lives together, if you like."

"But the house," George paused and looked round the kitchen and then, as if he had suddenly discovered that he was able to see through walls, scanned it a second time allowing his eyes to stray into the rooms beyond, "the house is just fine. We've space enough; bedrooms, the garden. And there are good schools nearby. I'm sure they would be happy here."

Florence looked at him almost as if the notion of happiness was new to her, or as if he might be party to the preview of some secret new equilibrium, a preview as yet denied her. How could he be talking of happiness all the while they had this burden of choice facing them, of deciding how they would spend their lives? She tried to assess what they would be giving up if they took the children on, the price they would need to pay. And, of course, the rewards to be had, for surely there must be some. But whichever way she looked at it, she came back to the same point in the argument: it was out of their hands, they had no choice.

For an instant — perhaps longer than she would ever care to admit — she wanted to say 'no', that she was sorry but they would have to fend for themselves, throw themselves on someone else's mercy. They were just children; they would cope. Or they would never know of the decision she and George had taken. The future was hers and hers alone; why should she give it up or mould it into something it was never meant to be?

"It is a happy house George, isn't it?"

Having uttered it, she wondered at the phrase, her decision to personalise mere bricks and mortar which — although she had been the medium through which the purchase had been made — was now jointly theirs. She assumed she would be nothing without George, and they would be nothing without the house. It was a statement made as if she recognised that there was a third party involved in the debate, a 'dreadful triumvirate' perhaps — though she had no idea how the house could possibly be dreadful. Rather, it was as if she could see it as the character which held the casting vote over that part of her which needed to say 'no' — and every part of George which, she knew, wanted to say 'yes'.

"It always has been," George replied, not because it was necessarily true, but because it felt that way, "and it will continue to be. Or perhaps happier than we might ever have imagined."

And what did the house think? If Florence had, in those last few desperate hours, ever imagined she had a choice, that there might be a card she could play which would sway the outcome, then her realising the power the house had over them, the thrall in which the two of them were held, meant that capitulation was the only possible outcome.

"You think so?"

Did George see the house's role in that way? Florence doubted it. She was certain that he was so firmly on the children's side that no external influence was needed. His was a decision — not a choice — fuelled by thwarted desire, and by not having a selfish bone in his body. If she had ever doubted his selflessness (and she did not believe she had), at that precise instant — the moment he nodded in response to her final question — all doubts dissipated into the air. George and the house would keep her safe. And as she realised that, she suspected she had never loved him as much as she did at that moment. Even so, if she smiled just then it was still a sad and reflective smile. She knew that — even had it been possible — she would never be able tell him exactly what she felt for him in that fragment of a second.

It would be her second secret.

"Well then."

VI

The image of Maddie's abstract painting now dissolved, Owen resumes his walk back towards the house and the iron bench. He allows his sense of propriety to be piqued by the uneven yew and the weeds in the borders, knowing all the while Maddie will be somewhere nearby watching him. Not put off by its current state of neglect, he assumes she has remained continuously acquainted with the place and is far too familiar with it to be distracted. For her there can be only one subject currently warranting any kind of inspection: her brother.

"What do you remember?" he asks, as if interrupting her. In the privacy of this little oasis cradled by hedges and bushes on three sides and the house on the other, it is irrelevant whether he utters the words aloud or not. Indeed, If you were to ask him how vocal he has actually been he would probably be unable to tell you.

"About what?"

Comforted she is still there, Owen is happy to carry on their conversation. He chases away the notion that soon she will not be — and for the second time.

"Oh, I don't know. Everything."

Maddie laughs. In its own way it is a laugh which, rather than transcend time, locates her in it, firmly and irrevocably. It is a laugh from when she was young — early twenties perhaps — and one of which he had gradually been deprived over subsequent years. Even though it cannot be so, it is the laugh of innocence.

"'Everything' is so big, Glen."

He smiles at her use of his nickname then looks up at the house trying to recall the curtains that used to hang at the landing window inset immediately above the back door and the patio.

"Why not start at the beginning then?"

Settling himself down on the bench and feeling Maddie beside him once more, he stares again at the apple trees and waits.

"The house's beginning or ours?" she asks.

"Ours, of course. I'm not sure anyone knows the entire history of the house."

"Really? I always assumed uncle George knew just about everything there was to know — even if he played second fiddle to Florence most of the time. I think their jousting was a public game they enjoyed playing."

Owen wants to ask her if she has spoken with them recently, seen them from wherever she is — ridiculous though the notion may be — and for a moment wonders if he might use her as a conduit to establish what they wanted him to do with the place.

"There were many games I suspect," he says.

"What do you mean?"

Aware that his tone betrayed more than he intended, Owen tries to rein her back.

"Oh, you know." He pauses, hoping she does not. "Maybe later." It is a meagre but sufficient concession. "But for now I'm interested in us, our beginnings. For example, you always maintained you remembered mum and dad, but I don't see how you could have given you were so young. Too young. Even I have nothing more than vague and blurred images."

"Do you think I lied about that — remembering them I mean?"

He marks the tone in her voice.

"I don't think you ever lied about anything." The statement sounds hollow to his ear. "Well, almost never."

Did he say that last phrase out loud, or offer it to her in any other way?

Prompted by a sudden burst of sunlight, he undoes the buttons on his coat and recalls how Florence used to love her little 'sun trap'.

"But I wonder", he continues before Maddie can say anything else, "irrespective of what we actually recall, whether or not what we actually did was to concoct images of them based on the stories we were fed by Florence and George. Florence mainly. That and a few old photographs. Who's to say if what we know — or think we know — is in fact true?"

"About the accident?"

"About any of it, I suppose."

"Do you still see them as figments of your imagination?"

It is a notion which perplexes him somewhat, especially in the way she has phrased the question. Is she not such a figment, right here and now? If so — and if she was privy to more recent conversations with Florence and George — then why wouldn't that ethereal possibility be extended to include their parents too?

"Figments. Ghosts. I don't know, you choose." He waits a moment, suddenly unsure of his ground, as if his use of the word 'ghosts' might have unseen consequences. "But 'still', Maddie? You asked if I 'still see them'. Is that what you think, that I've always regarded them as somewhat mythological, like characters from a fairy story?"

"Haven't you?" She softens her tone slightly, makes it more inclusive. "Didn't we both? After all, what other option was there?"

How old had they been when Florence started colouring-in those first few years of their histories? Did she begin the day she and George took them into Alma Road and set them on their new adventure? Or during the days soon after when their clothes and toys and furniture started to appear and transform those two upper rooms at the front of the house? Owen is uncertain whether he remembers any of that transition. In his mind a new normal established itself without any resistance — at least none that he can recall — even if Florence spoke later on of difficult early days, nights of crying. Perhaps school helped the siblings acclimatise in turn, he first. The imposition of an external routine — and routine distractions — created scaffolding upon which they could all depend, the four of them; routines demanded they each be assigned their various roles in order for a day to pass smoothly. And if this had been so, it would have been a regime which also permitted them to assign standard notions of 'freedom' to weekends and school holidays, claim their collective place in a universal normality. For Florence and George that must have been as novel as it was unexpected.

At what point had he been aware — finally and irrevocably — that their parents were never coming back? Had it come to him out of the blue? Definitively or circumstantially? Or had that knowledge crept up on him with stealth? And once he understood that segment of his past — indisputably so — did he tell Maddie or did he allow her to find out on her own? He suspects that if he were to ask her she would tell him — and that if she doesn't know she might make something up. Refraining from the interrogation of someone who, in spite of her claim and his supporting affirmation ("I don't think you ever lied about anything") might inadvertently end up an unreliable witness, he settles on the one episode of which he is certain.

"We have decided — your uncle and I — that you are old enough to be told the truth."

They had been in the garden one Sunday afternoon, Florence and George sitting on the bench, he and Maddie each laying on a blanket. Owen was struggling with Shakespeare for an 'O' level essay; Maddie was sketching as she always did. When the spring weather was good this post-lunch congregation had become something of a ritual. They both looked up.

It seemed odd to imagine that, if they were only now being told the truth, Florence and George might have been wilfully lying to them for years. If such a possibility had previously failed to register with them, its realisation was to creep up on him gradually over subsequent years and, in time, expand to cover a wider scope than just their parents. That afternoon he had been glad to be diverted from *Romeo and Juliet*, struggling as he always did with the language, the poetry. Having been told there was meaning just beneath the surface, his attempt to scrape away at the veneer of words in order to get to the gold was inevitably doomed to failure. Where Owen put his book down, Maddie simply paused, pencil in mid-air.

"Not that it will probably be news anyway." Florence corrected herself, as if simultaneously devaluing both her previous statement and the truth she intended to reveal. She glanced at George who nodded almost imperceptibly.

And so she had told them everything she could about the car accident and the nature of their parents' death. It had been as brief and factual an exposition as she could manage. She might just has easily have been talking about the demise of some anonymous people of whom the children had heard circumstantially, like a minor filler item on *The Nine O'Clock News*. In many ways it *was* like telling a story — "once upon a time" — though one without any moral quality. A tale with very little beginning or middle, it was all ending.

There had been a pause, Florence allowing her glance to stray from the children and down the garden. George's travelled in the opposite direction.

"But none of that is really new or surprising, is it?" He aimed his question at Owen, the senior partner.

"Not really." Owen shook his head. "I don't think we knew the whole of the driver's story. Other than that…"

He looked at Maddie who was staring at her drawing.

"So." George glanced to his wife.

"We just wanted to draw a line under it I suppose," she offered, only now aware of the anti-climactic nature of her disclosure. "Officially. That's all we know. There is nothing else" — another pause, this time less certain — "in case you were wondering. Or had any gaps that needed to be filled in. Away from the public account, I mean. So that we can put it to bed, as it were."

"But what about them?" As she spoke, Maddie seemed still intent on her incomplete drawing, her hand still poised. When she looked up, Florence could see that her eyes were dry.

"Them?" Florence's brow furrowed. "What do you mean?"

"Augustus and Alice," she said. In the presence of Florence and George, she had never referred to them as 'father' and 'mother'. "What were they like as people?"

Owen looked at his sister. It had been a question they had informally shared, occasionally speculating as children might about characters in a story. For a moment he was drawn to the play still open in front of him. What if that had been called *Augustus and Alice*, or their parents called Romeo and Juliet? Would that have made any difference at all, to either their story or the play? When he and Maddie had been younger they had debated what their parents had been like, creating the kinds of profile which appealed to children of a certain age. For a while Augustus had been some kind of adventurer, Alice a model and actress. These were safe caricatures for people they didn't know, almost as if their parents were Ken and Barbie, figures who could be put away once they had been played with. Such fabrication also felt strangely wicked and dangerous, offering them the merest frisson of subterfuge and undercover activity. And though they had gradually ceased to indulge their imaginations in this way, Florence's relaying of the tragedy opened doors to potentially laying other ghosts to rest.

"'Like'?" Florence was momentarily thrown.

"What did they do? What kind of people were they?"

Without needing to look towards her husband, Florence knew all eyes were on her. Maddie's question was open-ended, flexible; Florence could do with it as she saw fit, weave whatever she chose into her answer, fact or fiction. That afternoon she wanted to keep things simple; there had been enough distractions for one day, and there was homework to finish and chores to be done. She imagined herself back in the kitchen making the supper they would eat in a few hours, and, in the light of Maddie's request, wondered which she would rather be doing, answering her niece's question or cooking.

"They were, I suppose, typical young people. It was ten years ago mind — to the day in fact, which is why we thought... Anyway, they weren't at all like the young people you see out and about these days." She glanced at George who silently encouraged her to go on. "1969 was a time of optimism I think, wouldn't you say George? The sixties had swung all they were going to swing, and a new decade was on the horizon. Man was about to go to the moon. Everything seemed possible." Knowing the children had subsequently seen the Apollo 11 footage she paused, half hoping Owen would ask her what it was like watching Neil Armstrong's famous footstep. He says nothing. "I think Augustus was beginning to show signs of ambition."

"What do you mean?" Owen sought clarification.

"Oh, I don't think he ever cared that much about work, not really. And when you two came along — well, they had their hands full. But I think he was starting to get the hang of being a dad, and I think it had dawned on him that the more successful he was professionally, the better it would be for the family. Not that that was what made him remarkable."

"What did?"

Florence looked at Maddie, unsurprised such a question had come from her.

"Your father? Love of life perhaps more than anything. He was an outgoing, optimistic type. Glass always half-full rather than half-empty. He was a zesty individual, wasn't he George?"

She paused finding herself in need of a little moral support.

George obliged. "Without doubt. Zesty. Good word."

"And Alice?" Maddie again.

Florence smiled.

"Very similar. Peas from the same pod you might say. Of course she didn't have the same concerns about career as Augustus, but like him she too was trying to come to terms with what being a parent meant. In some ways it was a little harder for her."

"How?"

"I think in the beginning children always harder for the woman — as you may find out one day." Florence tried a laugh to see if she had hit the right note, but Maddie's gaze remained unwavering. "I'm pretty sure you two were it though; I mean, there was never any talk of having a third child."

"They were perfectly content with you." George added, hoping his endorsement would perform some kind of trick.

"And you've seen the photos," Florence continued, "so you know how handsome they were together. Cut quite a dash, as we used to say." She allowed her mind to wander a little, to imagine herself looking at snapshots of a different couple entirely.

"Are we like them?"

Owen brought her back. It was the kind of question she wouldn't have expected from him.

"Physically?" Florence doesn't wait for clarification. "Yes, of course. You both have elements of them; shapes mainly. Eyes, mouth, nose. You're more like you father Owen, and Maddie like Alice. Wouldn't you say so, George?" Again George nods. "As for the rest of it…"

And of course it was 'the rest of it' in which Maddie remained most interested.

As he recalls the episode now, sitting again at the back of the waiting house, the conversation seemed to fizzle out at that point; Florence managed to avoid any further elaboration, making excuses about needing the toilet or having to do something in the kitchen. And Maddie had been content enough to let her aunt off the hook and return to her drawing. It was as if she knew that now the genii was out of the bottle the conversation could be resurrected at will. Owen likes to think that he returned to *Romeo and Juliet* with fresh eyes, Maddie back to her sketch satisfied. Probably neither were true.

"You spoke of them later."

As if she has been attendant throughout Owen's recollection, Maddie's present-day voice intrudes and he turns to where she should be sitting.

"Of course. Don't you remember?"

"I remember everything," she replies with a trace of the mischievous in her voice. Her statement is much like that about always telling the truth, each in turn prompting Owen to smile at his sister's desire for memory to be absolute, unequivocal. Accurately or not, he remembers her penchant for words like 'always' and 'never'. It was a taste for the binary which for him never aligned with what he thought it meant to be an artist. If the same was true for Maddie herself, then perhaps that disconnect had been part of her problem.

"It wasn't long after that they took us to the cemetery for the first time was it?"

"Either later that year or the year after," Maddie confirms.

"Perhaps the conversation that afternoon and then the visit to the cemetery was all part of them demonstrating they thought we were 'old enough'."

"We'd always been old enough," Maddie says somewhat cryptically. "And anyway, that wasn't what I meant."

"What wasn't?"

"When I said that you spoke of them later." She pauses, unable to keep a slight edge of frustration from her voice. "*You* spoke of them later. Or to Florence about them."

"Ah. I see what you mean."

"And?"

"Yes, of course." Owen feels as if he is juggling something slippery. "There were lots of conversations with Florence, especially after George died; before that, she with the two of us." He hesitates. "And - subsequently…"

Maddie laughs.

"Of course, Glen." She waits a beat. "It's the 'subsequently' I'm interested in. So, spill the beans."

"What don't you know?" he asks, stalling. Then, realising how stupid his question is, apologies. "Sorry. It's just that…"

She tries to help him out.

"Why don't you assume that if I wasn't involved in any conversation you had 'subsequently' with Florence then I'm entirely ignorant of it — which seems reasonable, doesn't it? And you should also assume that my original question to Florence — 'what kind of people were they?' — is still valid, unanswered. Or at least to my satisfaction."

Owen sits back on the bench and stretches out his legs a little, crossing them at the ankles. His revised posture is strangely comforting, as is the vista down the garden. And feeling the solid house behind him offers an odd yet not unfamiliar notion of protection, as if it has 'got his back'. Still. He senses Maddie waiting and feels cocooned.

"We talked a few times I suppose, and about all sorts of things. You'll remember the conversations with her after George died." He waits for confirmation but none is forthcoming. "I think she was in something of spin for a while, trying to come to terms with her own loss, the new life she was facing into. That was, what, twenty-odd years on from the conversation about the crash and when you first asked your question."

"And all we had in between were snippets. Or that's what I felt at least. I'd probe from time to time, but Florence kept those particular cards tight to her chest — or at least she did when I was around. And uncle George said virtually nothing."

"He didn't think it was his turf, I suspect." In recalling his uncle, Owen can only conjure freeze-frame images of his slow but inevitable decline between that garden conversation in 1981 and his demise some thirty-four years later. "Augustus was Florence's brother, after all. I suppose his memory was her responsibility."

"And therefore one she could shape."

Owen ponders the notion, certain that manipulation of their father's image was exactly what Florence *did* do — at least until she had no reason left not too. The death of George freed her of one of those reasons, and when Owen was the only one remaining in her immediate sphere — well, there was nothing left against which she had to guard.

He wonders whether Florence's motives were solely about protecting them — perhaps especially Maddie — from the raw truth. Or what she might have interpreted as either 'raw' or 'truth'. Perhaps that had been the reason she and George had waited until he was fourteen and Maddie twelve to speak of the accident. But to not go any further? To decline to answer the question 'what kind of people were they?' until Maddie wasn't there to hear the answer? The first time she told Owen what she really thought of their father — her brother — had been five years ago. Having trespassed into his fifties, Owen had proved he could look after himself; perhaps because of that she thought the truth could no longer do any real damage — either to him or her.

"I suppose there's no harm in telling you now." That was how Florence had begun that particular Wednesday evening. They had just finished an evening meal cooked by Owen, a one-off treat that had quickly established itself as ritual. "Not that I suppose you care much anyway. After all it's ancient history as far as you're concerned. I might just as well be telling you secrets about King Tut or Clement Attlee."

"Secrets?" he had said.

"There you go, tripping up an old woman when she's too frail to fight you off." It was a standard ploy.

"Frail!" Owen laughed. "Show me the person who chooses to put 'Florence' and 'frail' in the same sentence and I'll show you someone destined for the mad-house."

She smiled, a mixture of knowing and gratitude.

"And I should have added bribery to the charge too. Coming round here plying me with your delicious sausages, those crispy chips you know I can't resist... You're a sly one young Owen, make no mistake."

Once the old joke had been shared, silence settled again.

"Augustus," she said by way of opening gambit. Just his name. "I'd ask you what you want to know, but you couldn't tell me. Nor of the gaps that needed filling in. It's the same story there I suppose." She paused to marshal her troops. "The facts you have, I know that. But it's not facts you're after. Or they weren't what Maddie was interested in, not really. 'Tell me what they were like' she asked me one day. Do you remember? As if it were that easy."

"You don't have to..."

"But I do." She interrupted him. "Don't give me that 'don't have to' nonsense. And anyway, this is as much for me as it is for you. If anything, I'm the only one who'll benefit now, meagre reward though it may be."

"Benefit? How so?"

"Oh, relieving myself from holding on to things I suppose. Things I probably should have told you years ago. Not that there's anything too dramatic — not in the grand scheme." She delayed again. "Think of me cleansing myself, purging my guilt, rather than paying any kind of debt. At least that's how I'll look upon it. Better that way, eh?"

He made to get up and close the living room curtains but was halted by a wave of her hand. Dusk was falling rapidly, and they had reached that pivot point where the window's reflection of the inside of the room carried as much light as that coming through from the outside. It was almost like the manifestation of a universe where two realities coexisted together, but only for a few fleeting moments.

"I don't think I ever liked Augustus that much." It was significant salvo. "He used to want me to call him Aggie, did I ever tell you that?" Owen shook his head. "But I refused. It may have suited some of the friends of his youth, but it didn't work for me. And I didn't think it suited him. Perhaps it didn't suit me either." She paused, and then fired her initial guns again as if she wanted to ensure she'd hit her target. "Even though he was my kith and kin, I never really liked him. I know as the older sister I was supposed to have had responsibilities as far as he was concerned, that it was partly my job to look after him, but there came a point when I couldn't see any merit in it."

"How old had you been?" Owen sought a triangulation point.

"I don't know. Fifteen? Nine? Does it matter?" She let the rhetorical question settle. "He was always a little too full of himself for my liking. Especially later on. Ours was a Quaker household — or something approximating to it. Not that we were devout. Is that the right word for Quakers? Anyway, this only made Augustus' flightiness stand out even more. Perhaps I had already been indoctrinated before he began to take shape as a person; maybe my reaction to him said as much about me... But flighty he was, to my mind at least. And then throughout his teenage years he became something else."

Florence stopped, wanting to be prompted. Perhaps having Owen to force her on made things easier.

"Something else?"

"A chancer. A fly-boy. A bit of a spiv. Flighty was supported by flashy. Mind you," she visibly corrected herself, somehow wanting mitigation, "he was charismatic with it. Quite the charmer. An attractive young man, without doubt. So you see how all of that — his flair and flash and magnetism — rubbed me up the wrong way. Perhaps I was jealous."

"And were you?"

Florence made a show of considering Owen's question, as if it was one she hadn't asked herself over and over across the chasm of years.

"Probably. Where I became set in my ways, Augustus was busy exploring. Did you know he was an active trade unionist for a while?"

"I don't think I did." Owen was unable to hide his surprise.

"It was one of the things he ended up trying on for size, just to see how it fitted. Or felt. And all that CND stuff. He was a salesman too — but of nothing other than himself. Although he was only twenty-one when he met Alice I think we had hopes — your grandparents and I — that she might calm him down or straighten him out."

Although he instinctively knew the answer, Owen couldn't help but ask the obvious question. It was required of him to keep Florence up to the task.

"And did she?"

Florence smiled at the naïvety of the question.

"Of course not. They were as bad as each other. If anything Alice made him even worse, and for the first six or so years of their relationship — right up until you were born — they were... I don't know. Dissolute, I suppose. Wasters, of a kind."

"You sound angry."

"Angry?" Florence weighed the word in her mind much in the manner as someone might take a sweet onto their tongue and roll it around to better acquaint themselves with its flavour. Or to decide whether or not they liked it. "More disappointed, I suppose. For all his faults, Augustus had a sharp and bright mind. Perhaps I also assumed he could do better for himself. For a while we hoped you and Maddie might be the spark that helped him see it."

"Isn't that how young people are?"

She looked at Owen as if she found his assertion the height of ignorance.

"I wasn't. And neither were you, thank goodness. Nor was Maddie — though she had her own challenges." Florence waited a heartbeat to see if there was any comeback on her statements. "But Augustus? Flighty, charming, political, careless, bad with money, idealistic or foolhardy (take your pick). And, perhaps most regretfully of all, dishonest."

Owen felt a strange ambivalence towards Florence's words; although she was talking about his father, she might have been describing anyone. King Tut, indeed. But it was not simply his ambivalence which disturbed him, nor having to interpret what she was saying; he found himself struggling to know how he should relate to such revelations. Should he have been offended at her accusations of dissolution and flightiness? And if so, would that have been on behalf of his late father or himself somehow? Or for Maddie, as if Florence's confessions might have some posthumous impact on her?

"What do you mean dishonest? That seems an entirely different category of accusation compared to being 'flighty'."

"It is, it is." Florence looked around the room. There was something almost nervous in her action, secretive almost, as if she had be caught with her hand in the cookie jar.

If Owen missed the subtlety of her involuntary gesture, it was because he had already settled on the image of her seeking out photographs that were not there — not only not on display, but never taken. He had been fifty-three years old, Florence nearly eighty-one, yet it was as if he had been transported back to that afternoon when he found himself on a rug on the lawn with *Romeo and Juliet* open in front of him, Maddie asking her question, and Florence — in this altered version of reality — actually answering it.

"He was engaged to be married. The year before he met your mother. He was still a child really; a twenty-year-old boy trying to find his place in the world, testing its boundaries to see how far he could push them. Rose had been four years older; a strange wan young woman who had been seduced by that charm of his before she knew it. Don't ask me how they had been thrown together, I have no idea; but there she was one Saturday, large as life, come to tea. There may even have been sausages, who knows." She floated her little joke towards him as if it might save one of them. Owen didn't laugh. "Yet all the while Augustus was still busy working things out, trying to shape himself, fit into his..." She shook her head, unhappy with the fanciful turn of phrase. "And all the time he was doing that, poor Rose was becoming increasingly besotted. When he woke up one morning and saw her for what she was — or saw himself for what he wanted to be — he simply finished with her on the spot. They were two months from being married."

"That's dreadful." Feeling bound to say something — yet still oddly detached from Florence's parable — Owen settled on a platitude delivered in a moralistic tone. Once out, the words suggested something more judgemental than he'd had in mind.

"Indeed. Augustus went gallivanting off, still gaily joining the dots on his personality, while Rose wilted. If you'll excuse the metaphor." Florence waited for its dust to settle. "And then suddenly there was Alice."

"And what did she say?"

"Alice?"

"Yes. About Rose."

"She didn't know." Florence made no effort to sugar-coat the pill. Then she handed Owen a second one. "She never knew. Never. No-one else did. We certainly weren't going to tell her, after all it was none of our business."

At this, Owen stood up in a second attempt to close the curtains. This time Florence did nothing to restrain him. The pivot point of light had passed; all he could see in the window was himself and the reflection from inside the room.

"Do you think it would have made any difference?" Owen asked, still facing his other self.

"What, Alice knowing?" Florence paused just an instant to consider the question. "It might have depended how she found out, who told her; though, to the best of my knowledge, she didn't know, and Augustus was clearly never going to tell her… Or maybe he did and I'm doing him an injustice. But I'm as certain as I can be that he didn't. Ever. There was the odd glance he'd shoot me during conversations sometimes — conversations involving Alice — which seemed proof enough of her ignorance. They were warnings to stay away from his past. It was off-limits and, from his perspective, that's how it was going to stay." Taking a moment, Florence appeared to try and attach herself to somewhere in her own history, perhaps to multiple incidents in the self-same room where she sat. " But to answer your question, I don't think it would have made any difference at all."

"Why not?"

Owen and Maddie had been brought up by Florence and George to value honesty above all else. Perhaps that was why Florence had been protecting them, afraid that their father's dishonesty might trigger an unwanted reaction in them, or risk proving or disproving something else entirely. Owen wondered if, as people, they would have been changed had Florence told them their father's secret when they had been teenagers, that afternoon in the garden.

Florence said nothing.

"I can't see how she wouldn't have been affected, or changed her opinion of him." It was a mature an assessment as he had been able to summon.

"But if she loved him too much, do you still think that would have insulated her? It certainly did no such thing for poor Rose." Florence glanced about the room, her gaze settling on the mantle and the clock sat ticking there. "I think Alice was too much like Augustus; so much so that she might actually have understood his position. Even supported him. And why should she revolt against his decision if it meant he landed in her lap?"

It was a phrase that suddenly concerned Owen.

"But it wasn't a rebound thing? Augustus and Alice I mean."

"Not as far as I could see." Florence allowed the idea to permeate before refuting it. "No. They were peas from the same pod, both vaguely irresponsible, not good with money."

"Flighty?" Owen suggested. Florence smiled.

"Indeed. But unlike my dear brother for whom Alice was the second gallop round the track, he was Alice's one and only. She staked everything on him and, I suppose, when he looked at Alice perhaps he saw himself reflected to a suitable degree. What wasn't there to like about that? So he reciprocated. By all accounts Alice grew up something of a spoiled only child and found in Augustus someone who seemed prepared to continue spoiling her, even if he was merely engaged in some kind of proxy self-worship. Not that either of them would have seen it that way."

Silence intruding for a moment, Owen looked at the detritus from their after-dinner coffee on the small table in the centre of the room and wondered whether or not he shouldn't bring the evening to a conclusion by clearing it away.

"They lived hard." Florence's words demolished Owen's thought. "Though I'm not sure if 'hard' is the right word, you know; but they partied often, stayed out late. It was a hedonistic kind of lifestyle I suppose."

"That doesn't sound like it would have suited Rose," Owen suggested.

"Indeed. And there you have it; Augustus' justification for throwing her over. Of course I didn't approve — not of the throwing over nor of this life he and Alice were leading. Not that my objections — had I verbalised them — would have made any difference. I suspect I had ceased to be relevant for Augustus many years before, and Alice really didn't like me from the outset — though she could wind poor George about her little finger. In her eyes I think I stood for all those things she abhorred: like routine and obligation and duty. Which, I suppose, made their having you — and then Maddie — all the more surprising. It was..."

"An accident?"

"I was going to say out of character, but you may be right. In any event, they did have you and that was that. The first year was particularly rough. Alice didn't need to confide as much to me, it was blatantly obvious. But then things began to change. I don't think either she or Augustus were much altered — not deep down — but suddenly there was a new perspective, a chink of light. And then..."

Later, when Owen was at the kitchen sink, Florence walked over and placed a hand on his shoulder.

"I hope you didn't mind all that." she said.

"Your telling of the story?"

"Me unburdening myself."

"Did it help you?"

"Who knows." She offered him a weak smile. "When will I next have the honour of your company?"

He turned to face her square on.

"I'm away most of next week. When I get back, maybe at the weekend?"

Florence nodded.

"Let yourself out, won't you?"

VII

"Does it make any difference?"

It is a question, dragged forward from all those years ago and into the present, which Owen now offers the garden, the borders, the hedges, hoping that in doing so its echo might bounce back to him as if it had being spoken by someone else entirely and in doing so permit him to consider it afresh. Whether or not he utters it aloud is a moot point.

"To us? I don't think so." Maddie chooses to respond in any event, either by harvesting some of that rebounded energy or by assuming the question was directed entirely at her in the first place. "But you've had longer to think about it."

Owen attempts to locate the conversation with his aunt — the one where she had spoken frankly about their parents — as if it were an entry scrawled in Florence's hand on a calendar that might have been hung on her kitchen wall: 'conversation with Owen about A & A'. That casual? He isn't sure.

"Five or six years, probably."

"And?"

He pauses before answering, almost as if he is still waiting to hear the question afresh, as if it has been reverberating within him all that time.

"No, I don't think it does make any difference. Had they died when we were older, after we had come to know them a little better, then perhaps that new knowledge might have undone something, subverted any assumptions we had made about them as we grew up. Assumptions made from the concoction of experience and innocence."

"Perhaps what Florence said might have subverted the personas they sold to us."

"Indeed." Owen allows a short gap, then: "King Tut."

"What?"

"Florence said she might as well have been talking about King Tut, her point being that we might have come to know him just about as well as we knew our parents."

"Or better than we knew them," Maddie suggests, "given you can read books on the great King."

"Touché."

From the corner of his eye Owen catches sight of a butterfly as it weaves its way down the garden, instinctively checking his watch as if that were the best way to define the season and whether the butterfly's appearance was either early or late. Or simply 'on time'.

"But as you said, had we been older when they died," there is a thread of logic Maddie wishes to see through, "then aunt's declaration might simply have confirmed what we already knew, what we'd discovered for ourselves. So again, no difference."

"But if we hadn't, and if she had..."

Maddie cuts him off brusquely.

"'If' has no value Glen; none at all."

There is a sudden hardness in her voice, and Owen wonders how many times she might have replayed things — most especially in her own life — inserting 'what ifs' along the way in order to examine unexecuted alterations in its course, the arrival at a different destination.

"Sorry."

At this point in a similar conversation conducted ten, twenty, thirty years previously, she might have placed her hand on his arm to tell him there was nothing to forgive. Yet when she had done so often it was to confess that it was she who had strayed. Even under those circumstances it had been an action which almost invariably left him feeling as if *he* was the trespasser.

"So, in our case Florence's narrative changes nothing. That's the end of it then, isn't it? At best it's merely colouring in; a little tonal enhancement to pen pictures of people we never really knew and who we can't remember." Whether it is possible for Maddie to note Owen's glance to where he imagines her to be, a caveat is immediately forthcoming. "Generally speaking."

An untruth or not, Owen now has a means — admittedly insubstantial and unsubstantiated — to trace the route of his conclusion back to its source. Having done so, it takes him no time at all to concede that any such revelations about their parents could be of no consequence whatsoever.

"We relied on her so much didn't we?" Maddie presses on.

"Florence?" Owen clarifies unnecessarily, knowing his sister can be talking of no-one else.

"It was as if she took on multiple roles when we arrived: stand-in mother of course, teacher, housekeeper, but also never quite relinquishing being an aunt. Was it me, or did she manage to seamlessly switch from one to the other depending on the situation and circumstance?"

Owen's laugh is a fond one.

"The older we became the less motherly and more 'aunty' she was. Don't you think?"

"But George was different, wasn't he? Tell me you think that too." There is a plea in her voice which doesn't go unnoticed.

"You mean he was always seemed to be our uncle and never anything but?"

Maddie laughs.

"Something like that."

Owen searches for the butterfly again as he feels the pages of history turning, unable to stop himself from looking over his shoulder half expecting to find George's face peering through the study window.

"He loved that room," Maddie says, demonstrating that even after these few unconnected years she is still capable of finding the same wavelength as her brother.

"I think it was the only place where he was lord and master. His sanctuary — if you didn't count the hours he spent pottering about in the garden."

"And always conveniently just out of Florence's vocal range."

Their soft laughter is entirely genuine, filled with love for the couple who saved them.

Along one wall of the study, rows of books rose floor to ceiling; and where odd spaces existed on the shelves, these were occupied by souvenirs from holidays and the ham-fisted results of school craft projects. Mainly Maddie's. Yet unlike many such rooms in other houses it was not dark, the light absorbed by the books compensated for by the large sash window and the brightness of the pale yellow which adorned the other walls.

"We'd had a fight over the colour," George confided to them one day. "Your aunt was determined that if it was going to be a study then it should look and feel like one, sombre and studious. But that was never what I wanted. The things you do in a study should never be dark, should they? Surely study is all about letting light into the world."

Owen and Maddie rarely crossed the threshold into George's domain. It was, according to Florence, "more retreat than study", and she argued that it could never be a sanctuary "with unnecessary people running around in it." She never indicated whether she considered herself an 'unnecessary person' in the context of George's room. Even so, as children they were invited in on occasion — or tricked their way in — usually when Florence was in town shopping or off having tea with her friends.

The window being near one end of the shelves permitted sunlight to pick out the brighter colours on the books' spines and thus create a somewhat impressionistic effect. George's desk — mid-sized, Edwardian, thoroughly elegant — was positioned part-way along an adjacent wall and set at such an angle as to allow its occupant a view of the door, the books, and the window. Beneath the window was an old two-seater leather sofa picked up for a song at an auction, and nearby a single Chesterfield armchair similarly acquired. George's 'reading chair'. Nothing seemed to quite go with anything else, but the overall effect of this mélange was in keeping with the variety on display on the bookcases.

It was the leather sofa upon which Owen and Maddie sat whenever they were in the room. If George remained seated at his desk they knew their presence would be indulged for just a short while; if he choose to rise and move to sit in his armchair, well, anything might happen.

"What do you do, uncle?" Maddie asked one day, the pair of them having been invited to occupy the sofa.

"Do?" George had looked down at the papers on his desk. "That's a very good question." He made a face exaggerating his contemplation. How could he adequately explain his job to two inquisitive children who had not yet turned ten? "I'm a teacher of sorts. I write things — about history mostly — and share them with people who might be interested in finding things out."

"We're interested in finding things out," Maddie had said enthusiastically.

"That you are."

"Do you write about the war?" Owen this time. "We're doing the war at school. There's a project about the Blitz and buzz bombs and things."

"That must be very interesting," George smiled, "but I'm afraid that's not quite my era."

"What's an era?"

"Everybody knows what an era is, dummy," said Owen, keen to demonstrate his superiority over his sister. She poked out her tongue.

"That's not entirely true, is it?" At this George stood and walked over to his armchair, settling himself into it. "There is so much to know about the world — too much for one person, in fact — that the best way to find things out is by asking questions, isn't it? After all, there would have been a time when *you* didn't know what an era was, wouldn't there Owen? So. What is an era? Well, it's a word for a period of time; and usually a period of time that contains the start and end of something."

"Like the war?" Owen asked, hoping to prove his intelligence — if not to George and Maddie, then at least to himself.

"Yes, you might say that. But eras are usually much longer stretches of time than six years. Like the Victorian era: all that time Queen Victoria was on the throne. Or even longer: the Middle Ages, or the Prehistoric Era."

"With dinosaurs!" Owen again.

"Indeed."

"What's your era, uncle?" Maddie shot Owen a glance to demonstrate that she now knew what an era was.

"Oh long, long ago. Greeks and Romans, gods and myths."

Occasionally George would read them bedtime stories, invariably tales from Ancient History. They knew of Theseus and the Minotaur, Perseus and Andromeda, Zeus and Mount Olympus long before anyone else in their respective classes.

"I used to love those stories," Maddie says, pulling her brother back into the contemporary garden. "Jason was always my favourite."

"Was that because of his adventuring or the thought of a magical golden fleece?"

In the brief pause that follows, Owen feels the breath of a slight breeze and glances up to the sky.

"The colour," Maddie replies, surprising him. "It seemed such a bright story. Not just the fleece, but the way the boats were painted, the blue of the sea. Do you remember those pictures George used to show us? I know they were just paintings, but as a child they seemed so much more than that. Inspirational."

"We went through phases, didn't we? Liking one thing and then another. Typical children really."

"And you, fascinated with the war; the fact that our parents were born in the middle of it; that uncle George became a teenager toward the end of it. You used to pester him to tell you about it, what it was like to live during the war."

"Did I?"

Owen's question is both rhetorical and disingenuous. He knows he did. More than that, he now knows why George had been so reluctant to share his experiences; they both do. From those early probings when Owen had been nearly eight, they'd had to wait until five or six years later for the veil to be lifted. By then of course their incursions into the study had become less coordinated, less of an event. Both he and Maddie would seek their uncle out — usually at Florence's behest — to ask a question or make a request: fresh leeks from the garden for the roast perhaps, or some apples for a pie; a question about a date, a name long forgotten, or about an event yet to come. Rarely were they all there together.

One day Owen had intruded on his uncle to ask advice about further education (he was in the process of choosing O-levels at school) when he was followed into the study by Maddie on an errand for their aunt. When they found themselves together on the sofa once more, George again abandoned his desk in favour of the armchair.

"New decade, new opportunities," he said, the broad generalisation triggered by his embryonic conversation with Owen. "Let's hope it's more peaceful than the one we're about to leave."

"What do you mean?" Inevitably it had been Maddie's question.

"Oh, Vietnam I suppose. Horrible war. And Northern Ireland — though I can't see that being resolved anytime soon."

"You know where you are with the Greeks and Romans, don't you?"

George laughed at Owen's joke.

"Yes, most of the time you do. But only most of the time."

"Did they have wars then?"

"Men always have wars. Think of Troy, one of the biggest wars of all. Ten years of it. That must have been indescribably brutal."

"As brutal as modern wars?"

They both looked at Maddie, George the first to then divert his eyes, momentarily taking solace in his books.

"All wars are brutal, Maddie; it's how they're executed that's different. The Trojan War was fundamentally man-to-man, but think of the Somme or Ypres. How ghastly that must have been. And the Blitz was no picnic, especially for the civilians who suffered it."

"You were in the Blitz, weren't you uncle?" It was not the first time Owen had dared ask the question — but the first time George had chosen to answer it.

"Some of it. I was eight when it started and fourteen when it finished. We were moved out of London when things got dicey, so I think I was lucky and missed the worst of it. Unlike many." He paused knowing there was a larger story to tell. "Yet we didn't escape, not entirely. I doubt anyone did if you look deeply enough into it."

"We?"

"My family." George looked at his books again just as Florence appeared in the doorway. There he was, a man turned fifty, surrounded by pretty much the entirety of his family: his books, and the three people he loved most in the world.

Florence leant against the door frame and nodded almost imperceptibly in her husband's direction.

"I was the youngest of five, did I ever tell you that?"

"I don't think you ever told us that much at all, uncle." Maddie smiled, removing all sense of complaint from her voice. "You're still a mystery in some ways."

"We may know more about the Greeks and Romans than we do about you."

They all laughed at Owen's joke.

"I had two older brothers, Archie and William, and two older sisters, Maud and Edith. One way or another the war took them all."

Florence emitted an audible tut from where she stood.

"That's a little bit dramatic, George. They'll be drawing all the wrong conclusions."

"Sorry. But when you've not seen them for so long..." George paused, perhaps wishing he had remained at his desk. If he had done so surely the room would have been empty by now. "Archie was in the navy, William the air force. Will was a gunner, flew in numerous raids over Germany. He was always coy about where he went — had to be I suppose — but we think he was in the raid over Dresden in 1945. And then one day, not long before the end of the war, he didn't come back. I was fourteen or thereabouts. It was within a few weeks of your father dying wasn't it Flo?"

They all looked to where Florence stood.

"It was," she said.

"And Archie?" Maddie felt guilty prompting her uncle, but there was now a conclusion to be reached.

"His ship — HMS Hood — was sunk in '41."

"Wasn't that the Bismarck?" Owen dredged through his memory of old school projects.

"It was. Hood was the pride of the fleet, our largest fighting ship I think — not that that made any difference." There was a sinking in George's words too.

"And the girls, your sisters?"

"Not much older than you when the war ended, Maddie. One after the other they managed to get themselves hitched to Yank soldiers who'd hung around after the war just long enough to find English brides to take home."

"What were they like, the Americans?"

"At first, Owen, I didn't think they were good enough for my sisters. "He glanced in Maddie's direction and smiled. "But I suppose that's natural. They were a little too loud, a little too flash." George's description was interrupted by a slight cough from Florence. Recognising the danger of drawing parallels with Augustus, he corrected his trajectory accordingly. "But once you got to know them they were nice enough chaps. Didn't stop them taking the girls away from me though. As the new decade dawned — another new decade, though now it's an old one of course — I was turning eighteen, Maud and Edith were heading across the Atlantic, and another war was brewing." Expecting someone to interject at this point, George stopped. When no-one filled the void, he was forced to round out his narrative. "Korea."

As if it were a cue, Florence stood upright and turned and left the room.

Whether or not Owen was about to follow her — he and George making coincident assumptions that the exchange was over — he was prevented from any immediate manoeuvre by Maddie.

"Was it hard for you, uncle, after the war, once your siblings were no longer around, your sisters gone off to America?"

George spent a moment examining Maddie's word 'hard', and wondered how he might contextualise it in the light of those confusing post-war days.

"You know, that's a very good question." It was a concession which prevented any awkwardness.

Aware that they had already crossed one invisible line, Maddie was keen to make the most of her opportunity. Where Owen had been interested in a first-hand perspective on living through the Blitz — a topic which, in the end, George had deftly skirted — she was keen to establish the emotional after-effects of the war on her uncle.

"You know, I'm not sure I've ever thought about it in those terms — even if those years are indelibly etched on my memory. Perhaps I haven't thought about them for so long because I knew they were always readily available to me. There's probably a term for that — and if there isn't I'm sure someone will invent one."

"Maybe 'readily available memory'," Owen suggested.

"Perhaps."

"And what does your 'readily available memory' tell you, uncle?" Maddie glanced to Owen for some recognition of her using his new phrase, but her brother's eyes were fixed on George.

"It was a difficult time." A frown that had been building suddenly dissipated into a soft smile. "Remember, I was about the age you are now. Not that easy being a teenager, is it? A time of change, of finding things out." He knew other people would be more direct, but George had always preferred subtlety — and from the grins on both Owen and Maddie's faces knew his inference had struck home. "Well imagine all of that against a background of rationing, bomb-sites all over the place, cities in ruin, nothing normal. You couldn't just jump on a bus or catch a train; there weren't shops open all the time; money was scarce. In a way we were still at war for years… Which is why you might argue your war 'era' was so much longer than just thirty-nine to forty-five. Against that kind of background, is it any wonder that Maud and Edith grabbed the opportunity to get out? They were offered access to a land of milk and honey where the bombs hadn't fallen, and offered it by young men who seemed to embody a new kind of dream." He paused, then turned to Maddie. "Beware of men laden with dreams."

Maddie laughed as if George's warning was the most ridiculous thing she had ever heard. Was it the notion of the dreams themselves or the possibility that there might be men wanting to share them with her? Boys had yet to become interesting.

"When did your sisters leave?"

"There were gone by forty-eight, Owen. I was seventeen or thereabouts, staring into an uncertain future. But in one respect I was fortunate: I was bright. Never underestimate the value of intelligence and good qualifications, both of you." George paused for a moment. "Universities were trying to kick back into gear. The war had knocked everything sideways, and once we were out of it the country was forced into a kind of re-set; one of the elements of that re-set was for academic institutions to push hard to get people studying again. So, as I said, I was lucky. I secured a place at Manchester studying history — which is where I discovered the Greeks and Romans."

"And the rest is history," Owen offered. They all laughed.

"Indeed it is." said George. "I was able to find a niche, make a small name for myself. I worked hard at it mind. There were some long days in the beginning. It helped that the University had its own publishing imprint; I got one or two things published."

"You must be very clever, uncle," Maddie said.

"Well, more lucky than clever I think." George's expression turned wistful. "But that was me in the fifties: working and writing, writing and working. I didn't get over Maud and Edith's desertion, not entirely, but the Greeks and Romans helped. I submerged myself in myths. Actually, as a young man I was probably entirely boring."

The laugh elicited from both Owen and Maddie betrayed their belief that George's assertion was not to be entertained. If anything, Maddie was now more in awe of her uncle than she ever had been.

"So where did aunt fit in?" she asked. "Was she at Manchester too?"

"Florence?" George glanced up at the entrance to the room to check that his wife hadn't returned. "No, she wasn't. And neither was I by the time I met her. I left Manchester in fifty-seven for a senior lecturing post at Canterbury. I was still pretty young — twenty-six or so — and being offered such a role at that age was too good an opportunity to turn down. It was difficult leaving Manchester mind; they had been good to me." Although Owen and Maddie had heard a little of this part of George's backstory before, they remained wrapt. "That's where Florence was studying, though I didn't meet her right away. The year after I moved there I gave an open lecture on 'Hera and matriarchy' in Greek mythology. Not too many people bothered to attend if I'm honest, but your aunt was one of those. She was in her final year studying Geography. I remember at the end of the lecture she stayed behind to ask me a question about Athene, I think it was.

Before I knew it we were the only two people left in the lecture theatre. When we got thrown out we went to a nearby café for tea…" His voiced trailed away.

"And the rest…" Owen ventures.

"Is history," Maddie completes the phrase.

"Well, it nearly wasn't," George's correction came once he had rounded out the obligatory laugh. "I wasn't — what shall I say? — very experienced when it came to women. I'd had my head in books all the time I'd been in Manchester, you see. And Florence? Well, I suppose she knocked me for six. I didn't know whether I was coming or going." He chuckled.

"I wouldn't believe everything your uncle tells you if I were you." Florence's voice broke into the room.

"How long have you been standing there?" Looking to where she once again stood in the doorway, George's tone was a mix of embarrassment and irritation.

"Oh, not long." Florence batted away any notion that she had been eavesdropping. "But just long enough to want to know how the story goes from there."

"But you know what happened next." Owen protested.

"Indeed I do," she concurred, "but I'm interested to hear how your uncle lays it out for you. I've heard him tell the story before of course, but you haven't. I'm keen to see how he unfolds it to the people that really matter."

"Are you really?" George's protest was a weak one. "How many different ways are there to tell it."

"More than you might imagine, Uncle."

They all looked to Maddie. Florence inclined her head just a little, a gesture that seemed to say so much — and which the rest of them missed.

"Sharp as a tack." Florence's words were, on the other hand, unmissable. "Bravo, young lady. Do you hear that George? Wisdom in one so young... So, spill the beans."

Although he knew she was playing with him — and that she did so knowing they both were on entirely safe ground — George made a show of discomfort before resuming his narrative.

"Well. Knocked me for six, like I said. Of course I'd met plenty of young women during my time in Manchester, though mainly students of course. One or two studying for their doctorates; one or two junior lecturers like me, though from other departments. But your aunt..."

Maddie glanced to where Florence stood, a slight smile on her lips. Then without averting her gaze, asked: "What was she like, this young woman?"

Florence stood a fraction straighter. George glanced her way then back to the sofa on which the siblings sat.

"Striking, I'd have to say. Confident. Really confident. Not afraid to ask hard questions; wanting to truffle out only the answers that would satisfy her." A slight pause as he resisted the urge to look her way again. "And intelligent. You can tell when someone's inherently intelligent."

"Sharp as a tack?" Owen suggested — which was met by a vague 'harrumph' from the doorway.

"The sharpest. And the kind of tack that shone too — as if it were made of gold." George paused, knowing he had gone far enough. "Irresistible. I was completely lost from the moment she asked about Athene and then suggested we go for coffee. I still am in a way."

"What poppycock! Lost indeed." Florence walked into the room and stationed herself at the side of George's chair, her hand on his shoulder. "He's no more lost than Stanley was. Or the astronauts going to the moon."

"But what about then?" Maddie qualified. "And what about you?"

"Me?" Florence feigned surprise that she should be drawn in as one of the subjects of this particular conversation; but she picked up the baton nonetheless. "Almost the opposite. I'd just turned twenty-one, and I'd already discovered boys during my first year at Canterbury. I'm not sure we called them 'boyfriends' back then, but there had been one or two."

"And, I daresay, they were cast aside when you'd finished with them," George jousted. "Hollowed out and left by the wayside. One a year I'll wager, if not one a term."

"Slanderous rogue." She slapped him gently on the arm. "You make me sound like some sort of...I don't know what."

Maddie interceded again.

"But what was uncle like? That man who lectured on Hera?"

"Well," Florence conceded grudgingly, "there you have it. He was clearly a man and not a boy — and a nice young man at that. I liked the way he spoke, his voice; and he talked a lot of sense. He was easy to understand and follow. Logical. It's hard for a man to talk about Hera and a woman's role, Greek gods or no. But your uncle made a decent fist of it, I'll give him that."

"Thank you, dear."

"I made up some ridiculous question about Athena on the spot, just to give me an excuse to see if there was any depth to him, or whether he was just another well-prepared young academic."

"And?" Owen asked.

Florence laughed.

"I'm still here aren't I?"

But now she wasn't, of course. Neither was George. Owen stares down the garden, the proof of their not being around in evidence everywhere. He wonders what it might be like inside the house, what hauntings there might be in her kitchen, his study.

"You could always find out," Maddie tells him.

"You're not wrong, sister mine," he replies. "And don't think it hasn't occurred to me. Not regularly, you understand, but occasionally. And a little often more, recently."

"And now, sitting outside the house, trawling through that memory of yours? Those conversations with George, the two of us on that old sofa just a few feet from here. Open a door or two…"

"I know, I know." Resisting the urge to turn and look back at the house again, Owen stands.

"I loved that old sofa," Maddie says, her words sent out like fishing lures, flicking the surface of a still pond in an attempt to snag a salmon. Beginning to walk down the garden once again, Owen is resisting.

"Probably in bits by now," he suggests, deliberately de-romanticising it, assuming she will be in lock-step with him, "or sold off. I expect when the house clearance people went through it all there were a number of pieces of furniture they decided weren't worth keeping."

"You mean you had no input into that? Told them they could do whatever they wanted with the stuff?"

"Hardly."

He remembers the explicit instructions he gave the company carrying out the work, the items that had to be saved and put into storage: George's desk; George's armchair; some of the finer pieces of furniture from the lounge, dining room, bedrooms; most of the crockery, but not that awful dinner service Florence had bought on a whim and which they never used; all the copper and cast iron from the kitchen; all the curtains and all the rugs, except the hideous geometric thing which had adorned his bedroom floor. And all of Maddie's artwork.

Owen senses he has no need to share this list with her, assuming that by simply recalling it she will see it too.

"Thank you," she says after a moment.

"For?"

"Keeping the paintings."

Owen smiles to himself, vindicated in his assumption of their shared wavelength and pleased to be acknowledged as doing the right thing.

"How could I do otherwise?"

"All you need to do now is to re-hang them where they once were."

Another fly cast.

"I don't think so."

"Why not?"

"Because if I were to rehang them I think I might mix things up a little, move that landscape from the dining room to one of the bedrooms for example."

Maddie knows he is playing with her so lets it go.

"Thanks anyway," she says.

VIII

This time he heads anti-clockwise around the garden: right-hand border first, then past the apple trees, about turn at the vegetable patch and back up the other side. It seems strange how doing so — and looking at the garden and house from this marginally altered perspective — can make things seem both the same and different simultaneously. He stops near where a swathe of germaniums cascades from the border onto the lawn, and remembers how George kept them under control, constrained in their patch. Yet he did so all the while allowing you the impression that they were somehow free to spread as much as they wished. It was a tightrope he walked with his garden, control versus chaos.

"But he was good at it, wasn't he?" Maddie asks.

"Masterful." Owen resumes walking. "But I don't think you and I realised that until much later; until we'd moved out in fact. I remember coming back and marvelling at the place, each year identical but somehow changed." He wonders how the boundaries of such divergent seasonal states are defined by gardeners, and when they know they are close to settling on something that will just work. "I suspect there were lots of things over which George had that kind of controlling influence."

"Invisible," Maddie suggests.

"To us, undoubtedly." He stops and looks toward the kitchen window. "But not to Florence. Never to Florence."

They had been in the kitchen, the three of them, he and Maddie engaged in the washing up, Florence putting things away in one of her vast cupboards.

George had been dead just two months.

"Remember that time we told you how we met," Florence began, "in Canterbury?"

Owen and Maddie paused and turned to watch her move to the small kitchen table, sit on one of its chairs.

"Once we had coffee I simply knew I couldn't let him go. He seemed - such a 'catch'... There was still a lot of pressure in those days for young women to marry early. The Swinging Sixties weren't that far away, but they hadn't arrived yet." She paused. "Put the kettle on would you dear?"

Maddie busied herself as requested.

"Which I suppose meant the poor man didn't really stand a chance." Florence smiled to herself. "Do you remember when we were talking about how we met and how he made a show about being naïve when it came to girls? That was rubbish too. Your uncle George knew what was what alright!" Her smile broadened for a moment. "But maybe he was ready to settle down. Perhaps that was where I got lucky. Maybe we were both a little afraid that if we let the opportunity go — the opportunity of each other, you understand — then we might not get another one. Or at least not one as good. It was a mutual sweeping off the feet, as it were."

Owen hung the tea-towel on its hook and joined his aunt at the table. Maddie watched on as she prepared the tea.

"We married the following summer. Augustus was there of course. That was where he met Alice. Did we ever tell you that?"

"No." Maddie's voice was a mix of surprise and incredulity. They both turned to look at her.

"Yes. Really." Florence looked at her hands, weaving her fingers across each other, then releasing them, then repeating. "She was somebody's daughter. I forget who. Your uncle and I were all too wrapped up in ourselves to spot anything else going on — though something clearly was. They proved it by getting married themselves three years later."

From across the kitchen came the sound of water being poured into a pot, then Maddie carried it to the table where she sat it down alongside the cups that were already there.

"Thank you," Florence said.

There was a brief pause as the three of them watched the steam rising from the pot's spout, waiting for the tea to brew. They all liked their tea strong.

"You mustn't let your uncle fool you though," Florence spoke as if he was still there, perhaps ensconced in his study awaiting to be served, his tea poured into the large florid mug he favoured and which they had bought in Siena when they had once holidayed there.

"Fool us about what?" Owen asked.

"He makes out he's not very good at things — all that rubbish about girls for example — but that's just nonsense. His way." She seemed to struggle with linguistic tense for a moment. "George was always sure of things, decisive. He never really showed it because — well, I don't suppose he ever needed to. As long as I knew; that's what counted for him. And I did. He was my rock really. I was only able to be me because of him." There was a catch in her voice which prompted Maddie to place her hand on Florence's. The older woman smiled. "Oh, don't you mind me. Come to think of it, I don't see why I should be singing his praises given the selfish bastard has gone off and left me."

It was intended as a joke. Florence's choice of language — given she rarely swore — was offered as the signpost of it being so. And yet there remained something lingering within the incontrovertible truth which, however relayed, cut through the language she had used when making the assertion.

"If I might be permitted," Florence began again, looking at each of them in turn, "it is one of my few regrets that neither of you were able to find your own version of my George." Owen makes to reply, but Florence stops him. "Oh, I know you've tried hard, and in your different ways, but having someone on whom you can depend... Well, it makes life bearable."

Maddie glanced away from her aunt and out through the kitchen door, heart and head focussed elsewhere entirely. It was a gesture Owen could not fail to notice. In doing so, he found it was his turn to place a hand on his sister's.

"Look at us," Florence said, suddenly lively, "sitting here with our hands linked as if we're engaged in some cheap séance."

~

Beyond the small patio area and almost adjacent to the kitchen door is a gate which leads to a screened and paved space where the refuse bins are kept. From there, a short path skirts the remainder of that side of the building before opening onto a grass section — little more than a verge really — which borders the rest of the plot, the house to one side and a series of boundary hedges to the other. George never referred to these two areas as 'garden' because he could do nothing with them: "too narrow to harvest, and too dark for anything to grow there anyway".

Although he tells himself he had not intended to stray beyond the patio (never mind abandoning the pavement) Owen feels disinclined to leave the house just yet and finds himself opening the gate — needing to push hard against it as the wood has swollen with lack of use and the relatively recent rain. Looking down at his shoes he realises how wet they have become from walking up and down the lawn, and knows there is now nothing to be lost from circling the house.

"You may as well," Maddie concurs from somewhere other than there.

The three refuse bins face him slightly askew from each other, and he cannot resist the temptation to lift the lid on each to verify that they are empty then rearrange them into a straight line, side-by-side, just as he had always known them to be. Whether such regimentation had been through George's tidiness or on the insistence of Florence he cannot recall, but as with many things about the house their positioning had been a constant.

At the corner of the building he looks up for no particular reason, choosing to attribute to his actions the motive of 'checking' — though for what he is unable to say. It is an impulse he continues to indulge as he slowly completes his tour of the remaining two sides of the house before pausing once more at the front door.

"To any ignorant observer," Maddie offers, "if not a burglar, you might look like a prospective buyer casing the joint."

He smiles at the thought.

"Hardly. I can't be a prospective buyer because I already own the place. And as for 'casing the joint'..."

His first phrase catches him out somewhat. Even after their deaths, he had never considered Alma Road as owned by anyone other than Florence and George; but now here he was, returned from his professional life and trying to decipher what might come next. He runs his hand across the door once again, this time applying a little pressure to the grime on the chrome numbers.

"Was it so bad?" Maddie asks.

"What?"

"Your 'professional life'?"

"Why do you say that?"

"I don't know.' Her voice seems to hover in the air. "Underneath the surface — and that natty coat and shoes of yours — you seem pleased to be rid of it."

"'Rid' is quite a strong word, don't you think?"

"Not if it's the right one."

Owen inclines his head slightly, partly to acknowledge both the status of the front door and Maddie's unrelated assertion. He cannot help but wonder if she is correct.

Standing slightly more erect, Owen slips his hand into the inside pocket of his overcoat and withdraws a key. There is a dirty brown label attached to it, the thick paper slightly curled at the edges. He may not have intended to go beyond the front gate, to walk up and down the garden, to circle the building, but he had come prepared nonetheless. "Take a key," the estate agent had said, "just in case". At the time he wondered if she was just being friendly, accommodating; but now, standing on the threshold, part of him wanted to know if her motive hadn't been entirely selfless; whether she wanted to see the house off her books, unsold, admit to a rare failure. It seemed a travesty if so.

"You bastard!"

Maddie's voice cuts across his thoughts. Owen laughs.

"I didn't say I didn't have a key," he protests, "though I had no intention of even opening the front gate, never mind anything else. This…" he looks at the key, then chooses not to finish his sentence.

In hearing himself confess that his intention had been merely to look from a distance, he tries to decide how it sounds, whether or not it rings true. But he cannot tell. Maddie would know.

"So?"

"So what?"

"Are you going to use it?" she asks. "Or are you going to keep us wandering around outside? Or even walk away, when there's so much left unfinished?"

"Is there?"

If anything, Owen had assumed that just about everything *was* finished. There was no family left, for example; he was the last in the line. And by extension, he had assumed the same of his connection with the house. On that basis surely the house — to all intents and purposes — was 'finished' too, ready to be erased not only from his past but from his future. Just like his career had so recently been, whether by choice or not. Lots of lines had been crossed the past few years ever since George's death in 2015, lines he had always assumed could never be breached. But now here he was, and here was Maddie again; what was she other than a trespasser? Or was that him? Staring at the sliver of metal in his hand, feeling its once familiar edges with his fingers, he realises that there might be one more presence needing to find a resolution of some kind.

He slips the key into the lock. It turns easily. And with the gentlest of pushes, he edges the door open. There is an exchange of air, as if the house has been holding its breath for far too long and is suddenly able to breathe out. It is almost like a sigh.

For a moment he hesitates again.

IX

Even though he was there just four years previously, that visit is sufficiently distant for Owen's immediate impression to be one of him crossing the threshold of a house which is both larger and darker than he remembered it. Removal of the furniture had insured the first, and the few remaining curtains being left partially closed guaranteed the second. Standing in the hall, the front door shut behind him, he allows his eyes to acclimatise to the subdued light before walking to the foot of the stairs unable to miss the silhouette on the landing above him where one of Maddie's larger paintings had hung. Casting his gaze around the hall he sees similar rectangular and square traces everywhere, and tries to recall which art work had adorned which wall. Believing he should be able to do so, he feels a failure when he cannot.

"Don't worry," Maddie offers, "it's harder than you think. Even I can't remember them all."

Owen tries a light switch but to no effect. Either the bulb has gone or the power is off. He suspects the latter, something which will limit his time there, the time he hadn't planned on spending in the first place.

The room to his right is the lounge, its dual aspect windows admitting light from both the front and side of the house — even if that coming through the side window is somewhat constrained by the proximity of the border hedge outside. To the left (also with a dual aspect) is George's study, and it is there Owen ventures first. Perhaps he has been prompted to do so by recent memory; perhaps that is the reason he finds it easier to locate the old positions of desk, sofa, and armchair. The wide expanse of the fitted bookcase stares back at him blankly. It almost seems as if it has been robbed. If it could cry out Owen is certain he would hear pain and loss.

"For you, that's very poetic," Maddie observes.

"It has been known."

But even the silent screams of the shelves and the soft resonance of Maddie's voice are trumped by echoes of his own voice, and that of his uncle. Owen imagines them in the precise locations from which they would have emanated, he on the sofa sitting slightly askew in order to face the older man enthroned in his armchair.

"You're sure this is right?" George had asked.

"In what sense, uncle?"

"Career-wise." The elder man paused. "It's quite a jump — and quite a commitment."

Owen glanced to the bookcases.

"You know I've always been a fan of order."

George followed his gaze.

"Yes. I wonder where you get that from." They both laughed. "But this, throwing yourself into auditing, and in such a major way…"

"Do you think it won't suit me?"

"On the contrary," George reached for the coffee cup which sat on the small table between them. "I think it will suit you very well. And, if you prove good at it — which I'm sure you will — the opportunity to travel is clearly there: America, the Far East. Why wouldn't that be enticing?"

Placing his own empty cup back on the table, Owen's attention was momentarily caught by the sight of Florence walking past the window.

"Then your objections are..?"

"Not objections, my boy. I just worry that it might prove too — I don't know — too humdrum for you. You might find yourself in something of a rut. I can't see much scope for imagination."

"Which is just as well," Owen smiled, "given I'm not the one with the imagination. Maddie would hate it in an instant wouldn't she? All that process, the black-and-whiteness of it, the right and wrong."

"And that doesn't worry you?"

It was a thought which had crossed Owen's mind more than once, but each time it had been summarily dismissed. There was something appealing about the regimentation of process. He had no problem with right and wrong — nor in telling someone when and where they had strayed and suggesting improvements accordingly. Honesty and integrity were two of the bywords upon which they had been raised, and were they not the most essential attributes of a good auditor? Did he not have the mentality and patience to be an excellent one?

"If anything, I'd say it was one of the things that was the most alluring." Owen paused, sensing he had somehow upset or disappointed his uncle. "Don't worry uncle; I know me and what I like and how I work. This feels like a glove that will fit perfectly. I would prefer to do a job I know I can be good at rather than one which may seem more ambitious but where I will constantly struggle." He watches George place his own cup back on the side table. "And yes, the travel is a lure too. Perhaps that will provide the excitement and interest to balance out any monotony in the work."

What he had not told his uncle — or any of them, come to that — was that he had already signed the papers and accepted the post. It was, he had been told, a rare opportunity to join one of the core functions of the business; indeed, a function upon which the long-term health of the company depended. And he had proven, both in his work to-date and in the aptitude tests he had taken, that he was prime material to make a great internal auditor. Bait or not, he had swallowed it whole.

"And had it been?" The intrusion is Maddie's.

"Had it been what?" Owen asks, turning his back on the bookcase and walking to the side window through which he can see the borders stretching away down the garden.

"Everything you expected it to be."

"Is anything ever that?"

"Don't be evasive. It's a simple enough question."

"As if you didn't know the answer."

"Whether I know it or not is irrelevant." For a moment Maddie sounds a little like Florence. "Surely the key question is whether or not *you* do. And if you do, then do you also know how that fulfilment of expectation — or otherwise — effected where you are now, what you do next?"

"'Next'?" He allows the word to swirl around the empty room; it has a haunting quality all its own. Years of experience have taught him that Maddie can be persistent when she chooses, and there is something in her tone to suggest she is in one of those moods. He has no inclination to put up a fight. "Yes, it both was and was not what I expected. The 'rut' George foresaw was undoubtedly there, but if it was not as deep as he worried it might have been then it was probably deeper than I expected. Having said that, the travel — America, the Far East and all points in-between — compensated for the routine. Much of it anyway." He waits for some kind of objection from his sister, but none is forthcoming. "So I was good at it, just as I knew I would be. I made a reputation quite quickly; not as one of those nasty negative auditor-types, but someone who knew how to do their job in a constructive and collaborative way. I think some people looked forward to having me assigned to their department or project."

"Which must have been rewarding."

"It was. Perhaps that was why I never left."

Although affirmative, the statement sounds hollow as if the truth had been gouged out of it. In the empty study the effect of such hollowness can only be emphasised. Almost as soon as he has said it he wants it replayed to him, spoken by another voice — perhaps his uncle's — in order to get the measure of it in a different register.

"Did there come a point when you wished you had left? Or when you realised that you should have changed jobs but that the chance had gone?"

It had been a constant source of amazement to him how Maddie could get to the heart of things so quickly. She had been like Florence in that regard. And now here she was again, still on his case, doggedly chasing him down, and all for his benefit.

"Probably. Yes." He wonders if it had been during that awful trip to Arizona. What year had that been? Or in Hong Kong the year before — or the year after? Looking back on them, his assignments had become something of a blur, merging together until there was just the one; and a long one at that. Had it been at their unrecognised point of amalgamation when escape became impossible? "Don't ask me to tell you when I fell out of love with the work because I couldn't — but I suppose in the end I did."

"'Love'?" Her turn to challenge a word.

"Okay, not love. But you know… By then I suppose I figured it was too late to change. Was that eight years ago perhaps?" He tries to triangulate: just after George died? Or later than that? Why did he now find himself having to navigate by the deaths of those he loved? It made him angry. "Maybe it was five or six. In any event I decided to keep plugging away. I figured I could manage another fifteen years, cranking the handle."

"But?"

"As it turned out I was the only one who thought that… Of course when the company was taken over there were lots of casualties. Some of my best friends." There are, he knows, various ways he can paint this particular picture. He wonders about trying the abstract, but is conscious Maddie would see straight through such a ruse. "When they combined the audit functions of the two businesses they found themselves with too many auditors. The same thing happened in lots of departments. Under such circumstances the staff in the company being taken over are the ones who usually bear the brunt." There is one more strand to the truth. "Especially when you've lost your edge."

"Lost your what?"

Owen laughs to himself.

"That's what they said to me, that I'd 'lost my edge'. Apparently there were more dynamic and thrusting auditors coming through; steely ones with vision, imagination." He shakes his head. "So there I was, finally undone by the very thing I didn't have and which you had in spades."

If he expects any comeback from Maddie, there is none. In fact he hears nothing. He looks around the room to see if he has mislaid her along with the brief spark of inventiveness that she and the house seem to have bestowed upon him. He heads for the door.

"I'm sorry," she says from nowhere and everywhere.

"What for?"

"The past. And the future. And for having to work it through again."

"What comes next?" he queries.

"Indeed," she confirms.

Owen walks out into the hall then turns left and into the kitchen. It is the same here too — the deceptive increase in size and the haunting light — and he remembers the conversation at the table, just there, where Florence had spoken about George soon after his death.

"She had less of a problem with my job than George did. And no problem at all with my lack of imagination." He aims his words vaguely in the direction of the sink, assuming wherever they are sent the room will absorb them as it sees fit.

"Aunt?"

He nods.

"Why?"

"Oh because I think she'd placed all her creative eggs into your basket. She always aligned herself with you and left me to George. Did you never notice that?"

"I can't say I did."

"Well." He pauses and rotates slowly on the spot. "I've always assumed that it was because she thought what I did — or perhaps anything I chose to do — would be unimportant. She always wanted to be creative herself of course, but never quite had the talent for it. Or the inclination. You were a godsend to her; someone through whom she could live vicariously. Even if that piled the pressure on a little bit."

"Don't you feel that's a little unfair," Maddie's tone is bruised, "both on her and on me."

"I don't mean it to be." Were he able, at this point, Owen would extend an hand to place it on Maddie's shoulder. "As a matter of fact I was jealous too. You had the kind of spark I could only dream of... It was hard enough for me to recognise such a talent, never mind strive to embody it."

"And it was hard enough for me too, the pressure, the responsibility. Not that I recognised it for what it was, not really. Nor its consequences. Easy to say now of course, when the need for a safety valve is no longer relevant."

Unsure what to say, Owen turns the conversation away from his sister.

"Would you believe me if I told you that there were times when I could have done with some help too?"

To ease them back to safer ground, he laughs at himself, remembers Arizona and Hong Kong again, then walks back into the hall allowing his eyes to crawl the walls and pick out the places where Maddie's work had hung.

"The evidence of your talent was everywhere," he says, just about resisting the urge to point. "Florence was the one who insisted your work should go on the walls, not George. And from the very beginning too. Don't you remember the debates you and she had about what should hang where? It was all a game in the early days, wasn't it? Can you ever recall George or I being involved in those discussions in any meaningful way?"

"That was just pride on her part."

"Yes, of course. But later on, wasn't it perhaps more than that?" He waits for an answer, then pushes on realising his phrasing may have been inappropriate. "We were all proud — especially when you began to sell some pieces."

"Yes, but not enough."

"Maybe. But on some basic level that didn't matter to Florence." He takes a moment to test this strand of his theory. "Or it was at the heart of things. I don't know. You were always the artist, I was the artisan; that much is certain, and that's what she loved about you the most I think."

"And George? Where does he fit on your peculiar scale?"

Owen cannot help but mark the slight tone of dismissiveness in Maddie's voice as if she is challenging him to prove his theory about Florence, George, her. Or is it more than that? Is she wanting him to use the house to justify himself; to see, in as precise a self-reflection as he can muster, his place in the order of things so that he can better answer the question about 'what next'?

"Think about what she said she liked about him. His authority and knowledge of his subject, yes; but all that was really about competence. The kind of competence he was able to demonstrate in the garden, around the house, keeping her safe. But having said that, it was his voice she fell for first. Remember? He wooed her with something intangible and against which she could only respond emotionally."

"I remember."

"It's all too easy for us to paint her — both of them — in a particular way, but that's lazy, just us responding to an image, the persona she liked to project. Surely she was a softy at heart." As he makes his assertion, Owen wonders how new this idea is and whether it has just come to him or if he has believed it all along — and whether it is even true.

"Maybe — but an opinionated softy."

Owen laughs at Maddie's observation as if it offers another layer of varnish with which they might coat their aunt's character.

Not long after he had taken the auditing job, his own character had come under scrutiny once again.

"Well that's it then," she had said, as if delivering a coup de grâce, "course plotted, all the way to the horizon."

They had all been in the garden taking advantage of some late autumn sun, the eighties soon to give way to the nineties. Both he and Maddie had come back for George's birthday, his fifty-ninth.

"You sound as if you don't approve," Owen said.

"Not at all. There is a great deal to be said for being able to see into the future with such clarity, such certainty. It takes away" — she made a show of searching for the word — "the guesswork."

They had laughed, as they were supposed to.

"I'm not sure that's entirely fair," George nailed his colours to Owen's mast.

"In what way? Did I say anything negative? Having such a thorough plan will suit Owen down to the ground; 'play to your strengths', isn't that what they say?"

"And eliminate your weaknesses?" Maddie had always enjoyed such combative conversations, particularly when there was the possibility that they could be at her brother's expense.

"Did I say he had any weaknesses?" Florence pleaded.

"Not in so many words," Owen admitted, feeling on uncertain ground. He pushed on nevertheless. "So what are they?"

"What are what?"

George offered a quiet 'tut' at his wife's game-playing.

"My weaknesses."

It was a phrase delivered light-heartedly, sufficient to generate another round of laughter.

"I'm not sure what the most appropriate word is, dear." Florence offered him her most ingratiating smile. "Vision clearly isn't a weakness because you've mapped things out so far ahead. And, in spite of what you may think, I'd argue that one of them isn't lack of imagination either, because you've needed imagination to come up with your plan. But having said that, it's something related." She let her notion hang in the air for a moment. "Maybe it's a dislike for grey. Or the inability to permit variation, or an unwillingness to leave yourself open to influence, inspiration, the vagaries of life."

"Oh, that's harsh," said George, though still playfully.

"Take God." If their attention was in danger of wandering off, Florence immediately corralled it again. "Do you believe in God, Owen?"

"I do not."

"And why is that? Lack of evidence perhaps?"

"Of proof, yes."

"There you have it," she said, as if triumphant.

"Have what, exactly? I'm mystified," said George.

"The fact that our boy here will not countenance the possibility that there might be a God. Am I wrong Owen?"

Still smiling, he shook his head. For her part, Florence's faith was somewhat seasonal, called into action at Christmas and Easter, and when her fortitude needed a little bolstering.

"And you Maddie?"

"What about me?"

"Do you believe? Do you concede the possibility?" Whether or not Florence knew how the young woman would answer, there was an undeniable confidence in her tone.

"I don't believe — but I haven't ruled out the possibility either."

Owen burst out laughing, then feigned hurt.

"You're just ganging up on me. Some ploy to make me feel inadequate, to take the Mickey."

"I'm afraid, my boy," George said, trying to be soothing but remain within the tenor of the conversation, "even if I declared myself to be unequivocally on your side we'd still be outnumbered."

X

As Owen walks into the lounge, faint echoes from that conversation dissipate. He glances around the room almost as if he is trying to track down where it went; absorbed by the heavy drapes perhaps, or leaking out behind them and through the ageing sash windows. Because there was always truth at the heart of such exchanges, there never any malice in them. It was a byproduct of one of the tenets of their upbringing — the primacy of honesty — which allowed accusations about the incontrovertible to be made without any fear or corruption. Florence had been correct: he did not believe in God, and could foresee no circumstance where he would be persuaded otherwise. And after what had happened to Maddie, how could his position have wavered since then?

"Really?" His sister's voice again, unbidden but there.

"Yes, really. Why should it be any different now? Indeed, why shouldn't my negative conviction be even stronger?"

"How about because you're standing there talking to me…?"

Owen looks all the way around the room.

"I've assumed that's simply the onset of madness. Or something hallucinogenic in the air."

"In the house, more like."

There is no way he can refute her suggestion. What made him push at the front gate, walk up the path, put the key in the front door? Whether that was inevitable or not — the machinations of fate, a sudden burst of imagination, or the benevolent pull of the place — Owen is unsure. In fact he doesn't really care. Perhaps there had been a time not so long ago when he would have been inclined to analyse his actions to the 'nth degree' (a habit from his profession bleeding into his private life perhaps) but those days are surely resolutely located in the past. He wants to assign his change of attitude — this 'laissez faire', for want of a better term — to the moment he lost his job, but cannot help but believe it may have crept up on him earlier than that; indeed, that it might have been partly responsible for his redundancy.

Whether or not the timing of any mental shift matters — and if he is comfortable with today's undeniably spontaneous actions — what does such a change say about the dialogue with his absent sister? The apprentice auditor who had sat outside that autumn afternoon attempting to defend himself and the decisions he had taken about his career would never have countenanced such psychological frivolity. Yet here he is, a grown man of fifty-eight, wandering an empty house that others of a more romantic persuasion would assert was haunted. If there were to be boundaries where new lines had yet to be drawn, perhaps where tangible reality bled into something else was one of them. Yet in a way Alma Road *was* haunted of course — but surely only in the sense that it was unlocking memory, providing him with a vehicle to see back into the past. In that sense one could easily argue that Florence and George could still be there. Indeed, that they always would be.

But what of Maddie?

"What of me indeed?"

He smiles at yet another echo. She is more than merely resurrected in his memory. She is somehow there, contemporary; he can talk to her, argue with her; this version of Maddie — who almost as alive to him now as she ever was — is prepared to joust and interrupt and ask difficult questions. When he finds himself wondering whether in some spiritual sense she still needs to be laid to rest, he recognises another boundary which requires a line and so imagines himself — one day — forced to draw one thick and indelible.

"It would be a distraction anyway," she says.

"What would?"

"Worrying about me when there are more pressing matters to hand."

"Like 'next'?" he suggests.

Turning back toward the hall his progress is halted by another intervention.

"It wasn't just that conversation about God."

"What wasn't?"

"Where Florence cross-examined you." Owen senses Maddie gathering her thoughts. "She used to do the same thing with politics. To both of us. Most often in this room and just when everyone was thinking of going to bed. Do you remember?"

He laughs. "Tried to get at us when we were at our weakest. Not that she was trying to change what we believed in."

"Really? I always thought she was more concerned about what we didn't believe in."

"Indeed." He searches his memory for a specific instance, but none are immediately forthcoming. "I think I used to annoy her because of what she called my 'small-c conservatism'."

It is Maddie's turn to laugh.

"Yes, she did pester you about that didn't she? Like an itch she had to scratch from time to time."

He tries to place his aunt in her favourite place — at the far end of the lounge's sofa, alongside George — but for some reason is unable to do so.

"And why was that?" he asks, ignoring his inability to conjure her up at this precise moment. "I never really knew. It wasn't as if she was a raving communist or anything like that."

"Nor a 'big-C Conservative'," Maddie offers.

"Indeed. But it was something she wouldn't let go; just like she chided you for not being left-wing enough. Do you remember, she had this theory that in order to be a great artist you needed to be politically extreme. It didn't seem to matter to her whether you were Socialist or Fascist, as long as you occupied some wing or other. On that basis — my lack of artistic pretensions, I mean — I can't see why she cared about me at all."

There is a lull during which the dust Owen has disturbed continues to swirl haphazardly about him.

"Perhaps in your case it was a bit like God; being open to other viewpoints," Maddie suggests.

"Or not feeling strongly enough about any of them. I never really saw the point of politics." It is a statement which — almost as if he had drawn back the curtains Pip-like to let light into Miss Haversham's salon — suddenly illuminates a potential source of their aunt's motivation. "Perhaps that was it," he follows his own logic. "In a way she didn't really care what we believed in as long as we believed in something: God, the Devil, Left or Right. Was it as simple as that, her mantra on all those occasions; was she just trying to get us to espouse something outside of ourselves, but something that was 'important'?"

"Her challenge to us was always to be the best of version of ourselves we could be."

"And maybe for her that meant believing in things."

Again the silence.

"What do you think she believed in, Glen?"

Owen thinks for a moment. He wants to be able to ascribe something definitive to his aunt, as if he might choose from a catalogue of such topics and find a few which fitted her glove-like. Unable to do so, he reverts to platitudes.

"Herself. George. This house."

"And us." There is more than a trace of regret in Maddie's voice as the dust continues to gently whorl and Owen begins to make his way back into the hall.

XI

The house was still. Although it had been that way for a number of weeks now — Maddie just off to start her first year at University and Owen his third — it was the kind of quiet to which it could be difficult to accustom oneself. It was the house's semi-slumber Florence found she struggled with. "It's alright for you ensconced in your study after dinner," she said to George on more than one occasion, "you've been used to quiet forever." Whether or not the accusation had any basis in fact, George declined to say; it was easier on such occasions to plead guilty. Having said that, he did know what Florence meant. For years they had been used to having Owen and Maddie there: at breakfast, in the evenings, at weekends. Gradually the early years of chaos had given way to increased calmness, shifted from frustration to interaction, from inane chatter to conversation and debate. It had been a journey for all of them. In some respects George wondered if the experience might not have been akin to them all peering down either end of a telescope simultaneously. If that were indeed an accurate metaphor, he could only assume the youngsters were looking at things the right way round, the future larger than the past.

But now — and in what seemed double-quick time — the children had become young adults and were away on their respective adventures. The telescope lay idle. Since the departures for university, Florence and George had taken their supper devoid of company, and tidied up the much reduced volume of plates and cutlery in as unencumbered a fashion as they had been used to all those years previously — even if they couldn't remember what it had felt like back then. George assumed somehow different. Even so, still they found themselves striving to fit themselves into the new rhythm, a discomfort which clearly suited what Florence felt to be a oddly mournful state.

"I didn't think it would be this hard," she said one evening in early October. It was 1985. She was sitting in the lounge, occupying the armchair Owen had commandeered for years. George was where he always sat on the sofa.

"What?" George put his paper down. He could tell from Florence's tone that she was in the mood to talk, that there was something she needed to say.

"Letting them go."

"Hardly letting them go," he said. "It was inevitable they would fly the nest. And it's only Maddie who has recently gone given Owen actually left two years ago. We've had time to prepare."

"I know. But it's still hard."

George knew what she meant. He had come to relish their incursions into his study and the conversations they would have. And his missed those weekend afternoons when they were all outside together. That seemed like the perfect mesh: his family, his garden.

"But they'll be back at holiday times, you know that. There will still be plenty of opportunity for you to wish they weren't here."

It was a joke delivered without conviction, though whether that was because he didn't believe it to be true he couldn't be sure.

Florence looked around the room as if searching for clues.

"Where did all the time go, George?" There was something plaintive in her voice. "Sixteen years, just like that. One minute it was just us, the next we had a ready-made family."

He laughed softly.

"Hardly our original plan. But look, now it's us again. Yes, we're older than we were, but neither of us is ready for the knacker's yard just yet. Who knows what'll we do in the next ten years — and potentially we'll do even more after I retire. There's a lot to look forward to."

Whether or not his words soothed Florence, nonetheless she briefly acknowledged them by smiling.

"But in three years time they may not come back at all."

"Why not?" George was evidently shocked at the notion, as if it was one he had never considered.

"Jobs; families of their own. You know."

Florence let the sentence trail away as she looked round the room. It was a gaze which had an element of reacquaintance about it. She allowed her eyes to settle on Maddie's painting hanging in an alcove above a small bookcase.

"How did we do, George? How do you think Augustus and Alice would have said we did?"

George, though confident that this was where his wife had been heading all along, was still thrown by the abstract nature of her enquiry.

"'Do'?"

"You know. In bringing them up. Turning them into young adults. Preparing them for the world."

When she looked back at him, for just a moment George allowed his own eyes to find the same painting of Maddie's before returning to her.

"I'd say we've done pretty well, wouldn't you?" There was no instant response, so he pressed on. "We've been very lucky. They're bright, intelligent, polite, and considerate individuals. We've never had any trouble with them — not really. They have their own unique talents, perhaps Maddie especially. And we've nurtured that; nurtured them. Protected them as best we could. Surely there's some credit to be had for a doing an above-average job. Can't we pat ourselves on our backs for that?"

"I'm not sure I think it's about us." Florence paused. "It might be of course, I don't really know." And then before George could stand to go and close the curtains, she arrested any movement on his part. "Perhaps I was most worried that they would turn out to be like Augustus."

This was most definitely not a line of thinking which had previously troubled George. Indeed, he struggled to recall the last time he had thought of his late brother-in-law at all.

"Really?"

"You know, flighty, irresponsible, unstable."

George laughed.

"I think we can safely say that Owen is as far from his father as it is possible to be."

"And Maddie?"

"Like her father? Or her mother?" He frowned as if weighing up some complex equation in his head. Maths never being his strong suit, he quickly admitted defeat. "Hardly. She's more artistic, so bound to be different from Owen. But flighty and those other things? I don't think so, do you?"

Florence stood and walked to the curtains herself, as if doing so bought her time to organise her thoughts. She dragged the heavy drapes across the side window and then the front. Then, standing behind the sofa on which George sat, simply said "I do hope not".

XII

It seems darker at the top of the stairs, so Owen pauses to allow himself a moment to adjust to the slightly lower level of light. Or is that no more than an excuse? Off the landing are the four doors leading to the bedrooms — Florence and George's, Maddie's, his — plus one door for the bathroom, and one for the airing cupboard. He glances up to ensure that the loft hatch remains where it has always been.

"Not sure where to start?" Maddie asks, her voice already beyond the top of the stairs.

"Does it matter?"

"Depends."

"On what?"

"Whether you're intending to go into all of them — the bedrooms I mean — in order to stir the dust."

"Or none of them," he suggests.

Maddie laughs.

"You never were a very good liar, Glen."

Owen shrugs his shoulders. Again he tells himself that he never intended to go in *any* of the rooms, let alone venture upstairs and across more personal thresholds. Yet he feels committed now; there is an undeniable sense that he should see this reacquaintance through to its logical conclusion, and in completing the itinerary perhaps resolve that undefined something which remains vague and just out of reach. Maddie's 'next' perhaps.

Immediately to his right are the doors to the bathroom and airing cupboard. Ahead of him, the main three bedrooms. "Well then," he says to himself.

"'Well then' what?" his shadow asks.

"Does the order matter?"

Rhetorical, Owen's question not only seems to ask whether significance can be attached to where he chooses to start, but whether any of it matters at all. Unsure, he waits for Maddie's intervention. None is forthcoming.

Perhaps illogically he decides to start in the middle.

He remembers Maddie's room as exceptionally bright and vibrant, and is surprised to find it little different to the rest of the house; there is nothing outrageous in the paintwork, nothing dramatic in the wallpaper. Of the two, it is the latter which unsettles him the most, less the mundanity of it rather than the fact that there is wallpaper there at all. Even though the built-in wardrobe is where he remembered it (George's early handiwork), he glances toward the window as if doing so will affirm he is exactly where he thinks he is. He notices a small chip in the window frame. Definitely her room then.

"You look confused," she observes, her voice wrapped around him as if she is inhabiting all the freshly disturbed dust.

"I expected more colour." Somehow it is a weak observation.

"You're not wrong. Don't you remember? You could hardly see the walls because of all my stuff — especially the year before I went to university."

Owen senses her reacquainting herself with the place too.

"There was a free-standing bookcase in the other alcove" — he turns as if being directed by a version of Maddie transformed into an estate agent — "and over by the window there were always at least two easels up at any one time. They would have had paintings on them in some state or other. I was being very colourful then." There is an upbeat lilt in her voice which seems to take years off her — as well as reminding him how much she is missed. "Then a little table covered in stuff: brushes, paints, jars of linseed oil. And the walls were filled with all my rubbish." She laughs. "You could hardly see the wallpaper, so it's no surprise if you've forgotten it."

He tries to recreate the image she has drawn for him and is only partially successful.

"Was that how you were at university?" he asks, shifting his ground. "I never did see you in your first-year halls, or that allegedly awful house you lived in for the two years after that."

Even though there is little that is amusing about the latter, Maddie laughs again.

"I was in the beginning. I tried to cram all of this into a room about half the size. The result was catastrophic. I used to get paint on my clothes, on my essays; important things would get buried under unimportant things... It was a joke really. So I decided to become a minimalist." She seems to wait for a comment but Owen makes none. "Pared everything back — even my art. In the first term I was a wild Fauvist, and in my second totally monochrome and small scale."

Instinctively with a preference the second, Owen cannot help but ask "Which was better?"

"Better? Neither. Nothing's 'better'." She dismisses the notion. "They're just different modes of expression, good for doing different things." Another pause. "I became all sorts of people over those three years, trying them on for size. Some fads lasted a few weeks, some a few months."

Owen is struck by her use of the word 'became', as if her art defined her. Which in a way it did, of course.

"And?"

"What do you mean, 'and'?"

"Did you find what you were looking for? Your 'style' — if that's what you call it?"

"Does anyone?" she asks, not expecting him to respond. "There are few people who succeed in finding a fruitful niche — and often these are the ones who end up being commercially successful. For the rest of us the journey is almost always more important than the arriving, I think." Owen notes the change of tone. "You can't expect to find yourself without discovering who you're not... Take Picasso.

Realist when he was young, then Blue Period, Rose Period, Cubism. Always searching, trying things out, reinventing himself. How can you pin him down?"

It is a fair point, but Owen knows the comparison is disingenuous.

"But he was a genius. He could have stopped at any of those points and still have been Picasso." Expecting an interruption, he gives her a chance to do so, yet it is one she does not take. "And you: Fauvism, Minimalism... I suppose there were lots of other 'isms' too. Which one was really you?"

He walks to the window and looks out, down onto the overgrown front garden, the half-camouflaged path, the rusting gate. Did Maddie ever stand here and paint what she saw through the window? He is convinced that she must have, and feels it a betrayal that he cannot remember for certain.

"All of them and none of them, I suppose." Her response is clearly a considered one. "I was always trying to find my 'style' if you want to call it that; not just at university, but always, and right to the end."

Owen wonders if she was tempted to say that she was trying to find herself rather than her 'style' — and if so whether that wouldn't have been a more accurate assessment. The Maddie he remembers seemed to have flipped a little each time he saw her: colourful versus monotone, vivacious or reserved, happy then sad. In the end there had been far too much sad. Was that — in part at least — a reflection on the state of her art, or did it work the other way round?

"Both," she says.

He finds her mind-reading disconcerting — even though that's exactly what it isn't.

"Explain."

She sighs.

"I would create an image for myself — mainly in terms of what kind of an artist I wanted to be, what kind of things I wanted to paint and how I wanted to paint them — and then shape my life to align with that. Does that make sense? If my painting was Bohemian then I felt I needed to live a Bohemian kind of life in order to have any chance of capturing the spirit of what I was after. And before you say anything, I'll admit that it sounds a little artificial. It *was* a little artificial. I suppose I was forcing it to a degree; trying to shoehorn myself into various shapes that might 'fit', rather than wait and see what happened. I didn't have the patience to do that."

"Why not?"

"Because, unlike you, I guess I wasn't made that way."

It is a theory Owen finds difficult to accept. In most respects both he and Maddie had been brought up in an identical fashion: to be self-aware, rational, considered. That's how Florence and George had lived their lives after all. If his sister was trying to 'force things', surely that went against the grain; perhaps in doing so Maddie was always destined to fail.

If she has read those thoughts too, she lets them go.

"I always wondered if there was a part of me that was like our parents — especially after Florence described them to us that day. You remember? More suited to me than you. Florence's description of them touched a nerve, struck a chord. You choose the phrase. And when it came to my work, some of how she said they had been — some elements of them — seemed more natural when I considered what I thought 'an artist' should be. I accept that some of the things I did were" — she pauses to find a word, knowing in doing so that she will disclose that she has been reading his mind all along — "manufactured. But they had to be. I had to find out, discover, explore. You were lucky. You had a plan, could set your life out like some grand 'to do' list and work your way through that. Which was fine. But I could never do that. Had I been made that way I would probably have become a draughtsman or an architect."

"Or a town planner," Owen suggests.

She laughs.

"God forbid."

"Was all that experimentation really necessary?" It is a question he has always wanted to ask her; one of those you continually put off because you believe there will always be a better moment to pose it. Or because you lacked the moral courage to give it voice in the first place.

"From the outside, what did you see it as? Or how do you think of it now?"

Owen glances back down into the garden as if doing so might help him find a suitable word. In George's day it had been neat and ordered, everything in its place, under control; his kind of garden too, he supposed. And his kind of life. But now? Now it was less a manifestation of his life and more as Maddie's had been.

"Turmoil," he suggests, immediately wondering if the sound of of the word he settled on was triggered by his vague consideration of 'soil'.

"That's how it seemed looking in?"

"Sometimes, yes." A stranger passes the gate. Having no connection to make them look his way, their gaze does not stray from the direction in which they are walking. And what would they see if they happened to turn their head, glance up to the window of the vacant house? "Mainly when it came to your friends, I suppose."

"Men friends, you mean?"

"I understand what you say about being a Bohemian, using that as an example — or at least I think I do. But did all of that 'experimentation' need to extend to men as well?"

He turns back into the room expecting a rebuke of some kind, but none is forthcoming. Not only that, but he has a sudden sense she is no longer there, as if she has abandoned him. He focuses his eyes on the dust that refuses to settle; wonders if in its whorls and patterns there is something tell-tale to suggest her movement rather than his.

Walking to the door, resigned to have his question remain unanswered, her voice stops him. It seems a smaller voice, confined to the far corner of the room where she'd had her bed. Owen looks back over his shoulder half expecting to see his sister sitting pressed against the wall, arms around her knees; it was her tell-tale defensive posture.

"It didn't need to, no. And it wasn't always the case that I chased unsuitable partners based on how I happened to see myself at any one particular time. As an artist, I mean. Most often my 'turmoil' arose from simply being crap at picking out the good guys. It was an affliction — and sadly a lifelong one."

"You needed someone like me," Owen suggests, only half playfully. Maddie laughs, responding to the lighter half.

"I wouldn't have lasted five minutes with someone like you. Or vice versa. All that control, knowing what you were doing, things being mapped out to the nth degree. I don't think I ever got that desperate."

Determined not to be offended, he smiles then continues to edge toward the door. His hand is on the door frame when she speaks next.

"That sounded awful, Glen. I'm sorry. I didn't mean…"

"I know, I know. And if it's any comfort, I couldn't possibly have lived with anyone like you either."

She laughs.

"You never know; you might have surprised yourself. In fact, perhaps you could have tried a little harder."

"To do what?"

"Find more" — again a break, this time for dramatic effect — "variety."

All three of his major relationships had been with similar women, each ending in failure; Owen knew he had never experienced what Maddie might have categorised as 'variety'. Thinking about it now, he is unsure of the nature of the logic which — having failed once — drove him to seek out more of the same. He had been beaten into submission for the final time the year Florence died.

He says nothing, hoping he doesn't need to. Maddie's defensive instincts allow her to rescue him again.

"And you know, occasionally these disastrous 'entanglements' of mine paid dividends. There were some very fertile periods as far as my work was concerned, periods when I actually sold things. Think of that."

"And who were these paragons of virtue who helped unlock your inner Picasso?"

"That's a low blow."

"Yes. Sorry."

Although he is now outside on the landing and trying to decided whether to go next into his old room or his aunt and uncle's, when Maddie's voice comes to him again it is still rooted in her own space.

"I sold a lot when I was with Dylan, so that was good; a few pieces that were Ricky-related. And I landed one really big commission when I was in Camden with Alan for that short period, remember? Alan — for all his faults — might just have worked out. He might even have passed your criteria."

"My criteria? I didn't know I had any 'criteria'."

"Of course you do. We all do. Florence and George had criteria in spades — but they were brilliant at camouflaging them under the veil of being wonderful people."

"Am I not a wonderful person?" Owen asks. It is an unfair question.

"What a ridiculous thing to ask your sister. Of course you're not wonderful…" He laughs, then the timbre of her voice changes. "Now it's your turn."

"My turn?"

"Your room."

He takes a pace towards his bedroom door and then stops.

"But tell me," he tilts his head back slightly as if he is addressing his question not to her but to the light fitting, the cornice, the picture rails; as if the house may know the answer to all his questions, "was it all worthwhile? In the end, I mean. All that chopping and changing; the never-ending difficulty with the inferior sex; what that did — or did not do — for your work; those hard times when you were down to your last few quid; the weeks of sofa-surfing… Or is that just a stupid question, considering?"

If he is hoping to be gifted a definitive answer on Maddie's behalf, neither the light fitting nor the picture rail show any sign they are about to cooperate. Nothing in the fabric of the place changes. Even though it is one of the biggest questions to which he has wanted an answer — certainly for the past five years — Alma Road remains unmoved, for now holding on to its secrets. As does Maddie who merely reiterates "your turn", her voice leading Owen through the next door.

XIII

Given he made a point of having his room painted every few years, its colours ranging through some kind of muted rainbow, it is perhaps only to be expected that the tone which greets him — something just on the yellow side of magnolia — is surprising. He wants to recall liking his shades bold and vibrant, and so, standing in the centre of the room, tries to remember each of them in turn, hoping that in one corner or another traces of the walls' previous lives might just show through. Yet there is nothing to disturb the pastel yellow; George was far too methodical a decorator to allow past shades to see the light of day. It is a colour — this yellow —

which, along with his not really remembering it, also surprises him because it seems relatively bright after Maddie's room. He cannot help but wonder whether the decor in the two rooms shouldn't have been reversed to better fit with their divergent personalities — even if, in the end, his sister's sombre wallpaper proved entirely appropriate. Then again, perhaps the magnolia arrived after he had left.

Walking to the wall in which the dormant fireplace is inset, Owen runs his hand over its surface as if feeling for history, imagining his eyes catching feint tell-tale marks where the chemical residue of some sticky substance or other resisted over-painting. After they won the FC Cup in 1974, he had insisted on erecting a picture of Liverpool's football team; and though he can't remember how long it remained there, he is almost certain it was replaced by a *Star Wars* poster. Imagining himself a Jedi was probably as far as his imagination took him.

Apart from recalling this rudimentary decoration, he has bizarrely contextless memories of pieces of furniture, rugs, boxes of toys; then, just before he left for university, a desk, a half-filled bookcase. Such things represented the transition between one stage and the next. He thinks back to Maddie's room and can only remember it as a single entity: a den of artistic chaos.

"A trifle harsh," she observes, "but I'll settle for that."

And even though in his old room, he cannot escape thinking about her. He stares at the wall which separates the two bedrooms, tries to project himself through it.

"What?" There is a degree of impatience in her voice.

"I don't know." Stalling, Owen senses that she is fed-up being the point of focus. Her words — 'your turn' — come back to him. "I was just wondering, all those times when your work wasn't selling..."

"You mean most of the time."

"I suppose so... All the while you must still have been trying to sell things, submitting to exhibitions or contests, striving to get galleries interested."

"And your point is?"

"What was that like? I mean, the hope, getting knocked back, trying again..."

To buy Maddie time, Owen walks to the window and looks out, the view from here only marginally different to that from her room. He wonders how it is possible that from remarkably similar yet shared views such different lives could develop. Perspective had much to answer for.

"It was brutal." Her tone is flat, matter-of-fact. "Brutal. How could it be otherwise? How could it not gnaw away at your soul? I'd be so optimistic..." She allows her voice to fall away.

Owen turns back into the room, scanning his own space for clues, as if he might alight on something which would make Maddie's statement concrete. Or make her real again. There is nothing but absence. He looks at the unshaded light hanging from the ceiling and then over to the switch. How often had his hands flicked that over the years?

"Not that rejection was something you had to worry about. Professionally, I mean." She moves them on.

He weighs up the concept, tries to take a quick mental skip through his cv.

"Only once, I suppose. At the end."

"And what was that like?"

"Nothing like your experience, I'm sure."

"Why so certain?"

This time it is an easy enough question to answer.

"Because I knew it was coming. Because I'd lost my mojo. Because I didn't care any more. You choose." Yet in Owen's mind this was not a valid example of multiple choice because all were true. He realises he is in danger of trivialising his experience, something which might inadvertently devalue his sister's. "I mean, at the heart of it I wasn't as invested in my work as much as you were in yours; it didn't matter in the same kind of way. That's why I asked about you I suppose, because I didn't know what professional rejection felt like. I couldn't know. Not until the end."

Uncertain whether he has done enough — either to satisfy her enquiry or exercise his responsibility for having had 'a turn' — he is prepared to leave it at that. In comparison to Maddie's life, his one rebuff didn't even make the same scale; it was like comparing a single fragment of a peppercorn to an entire chilli.

"That wasn't what I meant," she says, breaking the silence.

"Oh?"

"I was thinking about Grace, Lisa, Wendy."

"Oh," he says again, this time his emphasis very different, wondering if what she has executed was an entirely fair segue on Maddie's part. There is enough of a link to their earlier conversation of course: her men friends, his women friends; a commonality of theme. And she is undoubtedly right that his most meaningful experiences of rejection was not professional but personal. "What was your word? Brutal? I don't see why that shouldn't apply."

Sensing her settling down somewhere, he leans against a wall and scans the room, waiting.

"And all made worse in that you didn't know those rejections were coming — after all you hadn't stopped caring, and thought you still had your mojo."

He laughs to himself. "I see what you did there."

"Clever don't you think?"

"I would expect nothing less."

If she had been in the room with him, Owen imagines the obsequious little bow she might have been tempted to offer at such recognition. Having the picture in his mind is sufficient. It feels a little like a reward, proof that a link still exists.

"But you know the stories, Maddie, all of them. They have — don't you think — a certain similarity about them; a symmetry almost."

"Boy meets girl; boy and girl fall in love; girl leaves boy?"

"Nothing so superficial."

"Sorry."

Not that she is wrong, even if she didn't bear witness to the minutiae of each unravelling. The house saw as much of that as any one person, himself excepted. There were evenings when they came to visit — he and Grace or Lisa or Wendy — and sat at opposite ends of one of the living room sofas, the chasm between them as evident as the nose on your face. Yet he had been the last to observe it, certainly well after Florence.

"How are things?" she said one evening as he helped her with the post-dinner washing-up. "Between you and Grace, I mean."

"Things? Fine. Why?" Had he stopped drying the plates at that point, finally recognising the crevasse on whose edge he was standing? "Work's been tough for her, that's all. She's tired."

Yet it wasn't work Grace proved weary of, but him. Three years' togetherness evaporated in a single evening soon after, prompted by an argument over the political leanings of some newspaper or another; it was a crack which opened into a fissure and allowed the dam to burst. In what seemed like an instant he had drowned.

"Brutal," he says again, hearing the real-time word reverberate around the room; a room in which he had grown up and always felt secure. And how about now, with Maddie there again, raking over old coals?

"I never really liked Grace," she says out of the blue. "Nor Lisa, come to that."

"Now you tell me!"

"Lisa was always going to be a mistake Glen; why couldn't you see that?"

"Because I was blind?"

He wants to say 'because I was in love' but knows how hollow that would sound, how trite, like a get-out clause that never unpicks the lock. Even so, he still believes it to be the case; and that he loved Lisa too. How could he not? Perhaps if he were to admit she mattered less to him than he had thought at the time then the pain of her betrayal would be somehow lessened.

"Because you thought you were in love." Maddie says it for him. "And make no mistake, Lisa was the kind of woman who could do that, make you fall in love with them. I came across lots of examples; fought some of them too. Women who exude something irresistible, something that would make you a fortune if you could bottle it. Men don't stand a chance with women like that especially if..." She stops.

"If what?"

"If they're on the rebound." She hurries on. "And you were on the rebound, brother mine, even if you thought you weren't. You hadn't got over Grace when Lisa waltzed into your life."

"Only to waltz right out of it a couple of years later. And with one of my best friends, just to twist the knife."

The dénouement with Lisa had been similarly dramatic and catastrophic, which — given Owen didn't go in for overt shows of emotion — only made it all the more painful.

"Brutal," Maddie suggests again, re-emphasising the parallel she had known was there all along.

As Owen pushes himself away from the wall to stand by the window once again, he wonders whether Maddie had always wanted to perform some kind of emotional exorcism on him but ran out of road before she had been able to do so. Or perhaps it is the house trying to help him cleanse himself. Or itself.

"You'd think I would have learned my lesson," he says as he watches two cars drive past outside. He wonders what prospective buyers might have thought of the house when they first encountered it, whether they had any sense of the history cocooned within it, or even the power of the place. But power to do what?

"I had high hopes for Wendy," Maddie says — though if this is intended to soften the blow it can only achieve the opposite. "She seemed so right for you."

"Tell me about it."

She ignores the rhetorical directive.

"This doesn't work like that."

"What is 'this', exactly?" Owen, once more unsure whether he has voiced the question aloud, aims it more at the empty air than the spirit of a sister who has opened a chink from which confusion has blithely walked.

Never mind Grace or Lisa or Wendy, what is he doing here, standing in his old bedroom, haunting the house in which he grew up, examining the walls, the views from the windows, wondering about posters and paint colours? Did he know when he pulled the key from his coat pocket exactly what he would be stepping in to? Or even earlier than that with the estate agent? "I just want one last look around the place," he had said, trying to strike a tone of farewell rather than one of reacquaintance. Had he done so for the benefit of the agent or himself? Had it been a lie unconsciously told? Whatever the motivation, he couldn't deny that he was standing in his old bedroom — the one he had finally vacated some thirty-seven years previously — and was looking back on his eight-year relationship with Wendy. If he had felt a little like Peter Pan during those years it was never because he was the one endowed with magic but rather because Wendy was. It seemed she had the capability to whisk him away into grand adventures, almost as if she possessed a key which could unlock anything she chose, including his frozen heart. He used to fantasise about her finding him encased in a block of ice or a chunk of granite, and whether she thawed him out or chipped away at the superfluous rock, sooner or later there he was, living and breathing again, blood coursing through his veins. More than once during those first few years of the twenty-first century he felt as if he had been reborn.

"And then?" Maddie seems determined to have him walk her through the crisis. "I came back one weekend to find you here without her."

"Because she had gone. And it was my own stupid fault. Gone because I didn't have the imagination to conceive of fresh possibilities; because I was too comfortable with what I had." Owen turns and leans back against the window cill. "And what made the whole episode even more incongruous was that I was so well travelled. I knew America; I liked the place. And yet when she said she'd got a posting to San Francisco and wanted us to go, I said no. For no good reason, I said no."

"You were afraid."

"Was I?"

"Because you'd found what you'd wanted — after Grace and Lisa, and after all that time — and you didn't want to risk losing it."

"You may be right." He is unable to keep the bitterness from his voice. "But if so, in trying to protect that I achieved the complete opposite and threw it all away."

"You didn't think she'd go?"

"No, I didn't. We'd talked about getting married, having children before it was too late. Talked about moving too - though just to somewhere more convenient, appropriate." He looks around the room again. "I think I wanted a place like this; somewhere safe and secure; somewhere our children could grow up as happily as I had. As we had."

As his eyes travel around the ceiling cornice he notices a small crack in the plaster in one corner, and he wonders how long it has been there and whether there were other cracks in other rooms, ones he had yet to notice.

"There are a few," Maddie says, as if that will stop his fruitless search. "It's an old house. We're older people; we have our cracks too." She allows a pause. "Or at least you do."

"Thanks."

A strange kind of silence settles on the room. Owen closes his eyes and breathes deeply.

"Are you sure? It's probably not too late." Florence was standing again at the front door, her hand on his arm, his body already part-turned and over the threshold, ready to make his escape.

"I think it is," he had said. "How can you come back from that, when you've already stepped across an invisible line, stated your position? And even if Wendy took me back — took me with her to America — wouldn't she always be wondering when I might go off-script again? How could she possibly trust me after this?"

Florence removed her hand to rest it against the frame of the door.

"Do you think you can trust yourself?" she said. It had been ambiguous perhaps, but the emphasis was sufficient to place responsibility back on his shoulders.

It was enough to root him where he stood. He had glanced up to where the window of his old room was inset in the brickwork.

"Who knows?" He had smiled at Florence, a sad resigned kind of smile. "Perhaps it will be best if in the future I avoid putting myself in situations where that will ever become a live question."

"And now?" Maddie says, breaking into his memory as if she has been eavesdropping on history. "Is it a question now?"

Owen tries to reconcile those old words with a more general notion, parallels the situation fifteen years ago with where he is now. They are such very different realities. There is no Wendy to set him free; no job to tie him down. He has a past filled with memories and events, with incidents and accidents and a list of victories and humiliations. And a future yawning featureless before him.

"How can you know, Maddie? How can you tell if you're in a place where self-trust is a consideration, or even an issue? I'm just an unemployed man walking around an empty house unsure what he's going to do after he's walked out through the front door for the last time."

"I'd say that you're absolutely where you need to be in order to decide whether or not you're going to trust yourself — or anything or anyone else — again."

"You sound certain."

"I should do, because I know."

Feeling unaccountably tired, Owen looks around the room as if the very act of doing so will magic a chair from thin air. When it doesn't, his only option is to return to leaning against the windowsill. He wonders about lifting the lower sash to allow some fresh air in; it would surely be good to breathe a little life into the place. But he is worried he will forget he has done so, and leave the house with the window open and therefore vulnerable. Not wanting that, it remains closed and he resigns himself to the gently swirling dust, the slightly musty smell. In any event, Maddie is requiring his attention.

"Because that's what I had to do for the best part of thirty years." She carries on as if there has been no break in the conversation. "Whether or not I had been lured into a false sense of security at least partly because of Florence's constant encouragement, once I got to university I discovered that art was really competitive. I'd been so used to being told how clever I was, my paintings on every wall I looked at, that I took my ability all for granted."

"You discovered you weren't as talented as you thought?"

"I prefer to think that I found out everyone else was good too." There is a momentary shortness in her tone. "It was quite a shock. Not only that, but also I'd naïvely assumed my three years there would gift me some kind of serene passage through to my graduation and all the triumphs that would inevitably follow on from that. I wasn't expecting — setbacks." As she pauses, Owen adjusts his stance slightly, crossing his legs at his ankles. The room remains unmoved. "My work suffered in the first term; I'm sure of that. All the other stuff that was new didn't help: adjusting to student life, independence…"

"Men," Owen suggests.

"Boys." Maddie bats his interruption away contemptuously. "There were no men at uni — not among the students anyway." Her statement is both all-encompassing and a little cryptic. "It soon felt as if I was slipping behind, and I didn't know how to handle that. I started copying the work of some of my peers who I knew were doing well — which only made matters worse. Then one day my tutor asked me what had happened to the Madeleine who'd walked through the door on the first day. I didn't think he meant me of course, but my work. Jarvis, his name was. He told me to go and reacquaint myself with her, and that I had to 'trust myself'."

"Ah."

"So I did. Or at least I tried to, even if something in the foundations had already been put under pressure. I needed to remember where I was comfortable, where I thought I was at my best. My work started to get better. It was an important lesson. Ever since then, whenever I flagged, I always recalled what Jarvis had said to me. It became a kind of mantra, something constructive to hang on to. Or at least not *de*structive." She pauses. "So when I tell you that you need to trust yourself, it's because I know you have to; I've seen the power of that."

He has no reason to doubt her, yet cannot help but acknowledge that at some point history has demonstrated Maddie's self-reliance failed her; there would have been a moment when she had nothing more she could offer herself the well having been bled dry. What was left for her then? What did she have to fall back on? Under such circumstances how could she not seek solutions elsewhere? These are questions to which he knows most of the answers — and wishes he didn't.

But what of him now? What did he have to cling to? There was no art, no special skill or talent; he was, as far as he could see, just a 'normal' man. On that basis — Jarvis notwithstanding — in what should he place his trust?

He looks around the room once again. In addition to the crack he has recently noticed, there is a piece of picture rail which might warrant repair, a floorboard in the far corner that could do with a couple of extra nails in to knock it back to level. Those are the sorts of things he believes he can do — though admittedly not as well as George — yet surely they are hardly skills in which to entrust his future.

"And there's one more piece of advice." Maddie breaks into the silence just as he assumes she has finished her tale.

"From Jarvis?" he asks, if only to prove he has been listening.

"No, from me."

"Which is?"

"Never lie to yourself." She waits a moment — he assumes to allow him to interject, which he does not — than carries on. "I tried to trust in myself again, yes; but when I didn't get the results I wanted or thought were somehow owed me, I started to make up excuses as to why they hadn't been forthcoming. Not getting into a gallery or being shortlisted for a competition wasn't down to any flaw in my work but some other factor. I used to rewrite things or imagine rewriting things — reality, history, even letters I'd been sent — in order to make rejection more palatable. At times it was like being trapped in a crazy reality. But it proved enough of a salve to allow me to lurch from one failure to the next, do whatever I needed to do to pick myself up and dust myself off… But in the end there's only so much of that you can take, a point where it ceases to be an effective strategy. Or even a viable one. So don't do it, Glen."

There is no way he can counter this, so he lets it go unmolested. How Maddie's advice might relate to him he isn't sure, yet he cannot deny how profound it is, nor how painful the lessons must have been which has now led her to a conclusion which has arrived too late. In pursuing a volatile cocktail of self-trust blended with self-deception, had she not realised she could only be storing up problems for the future? The pressure could only grow.

Yet surely his circumstance is vastly different? When it came to women — the topic which had started this particular round of cut-and-thrust — he had deliberately *ceased* to trust himself, taken himself out of the game in order to ensure further rejection was never a possibility. Isn't this position diametrically opposed to that his sister had adopted in relation to her art? He withdrew, she threw herself in further. Irrespective of that, 'now' remains the unanswered question. Surely the future he faces doesn't require any degree of self-trust beyond the everyday; surely there is no circumstance which is forcing him to lie to himself.

Walking out of his room, he takes a moment to lean on the balustrade and look down the stairs. Half-way up they double back on themselves such that from his present position he is faced with the large expanse of wall above the half-landing. Just out of sight on the ground floor are the entrances to both the kitchen and George's study.

"Do you remember the piece that hung there the longest?" Maddie asks from somewhere nearby.

Owen looks straight ahead and tries to project back ten, twenty years. He recalls an unusually tall painting which, although the colours were vibrant, possessed a palette that seemed strangely dark, almost claustrophobic.

"It was tall and thin wasn't it? Seemed to fit the space really well from what I recall. Did you paint it especially?"

"It was my attempt at something Pre-Raphaelite," she says, knowing no further explanation should be necessary. "I was never entirely satisfied with it of course, but Florence seemed to like it."

"Inevitably." It is said without malice. Owen looks around the stairwell and then back to the wall opposite. "I think that was one of the things I missed most when I left the house," he says after a moment's further thought.

"What?"

"Your paintings. When I went to Uni, and then after that, I seemed to leave all kinds adornment behind. The first few places I lived in were rented and so they wouldn't let tenants stick things on the walls. And then Grace was all white and clean lines; she hated to have anything clutter up the place, and that went for the walls too. Lisa was similar I suppose."

"And Wendy?"

He casts his mind back to the two houses they had shared, tries to take a mental tour of them, identify their stand-out items of decoration. Mainly he remembers furniture, but there were splashes of other colour here and there.

"She was a little more 'arty' I suppose. We had the odd poster on the wall, prints, that kind of thing. I'm sure you could have swayed her, educated her, persuaded her to indulge a little more. She would have been open to that."

"Didn't she think I was a bit of a hippy?"

Owen laughs. "She never said that. Not to my face anyway. And even if she did, she still liked you."

He is pleased Maddie lets it go.

"What else do you miss," she asks.

"About Wendy?"

"No, about the house. In addition to my paintings of course. You've lived in numerous houses all over the place; surely

Alma Road was always the reference point, the benchmark against which other dwellings were measured. What did you say about you and Wendy: that you imagined your children growing up in a place like this?"

Had he said that? He tries to remember.

"Perhaps not exactly like this, but certainly feeling like it. Or embodying what it stood for." He lets the sentence settle before returning to her question. "So what else do I miss — other than your daubings?" Somewhere he hears her chuckle. "The solidity of the place, I suppose. The way it made you feel secure. And the rooms; all the right size, the right proportions. They seemed to work, to flow into each other really well. And — if we're being romantic — I miss the views from the windows. And George's garden. Partly for being the garden that it was, but also as a space that we could enjoy, inhabit, sit in, talk in." More recollections of conversations and individual moments come back to him, and the house is always there in each and every one: a particular room, the garden. He tries to shake himself. "But isn't that pretty much true for everyone? I mean, we all leave home, go away, build our new lives; and new lives mean new places, new houses, the start of other cycles, other chapters."

"Some people don't," she suggests.

"Don't what?"

"Leave home. Not many, I'll admit; but some. A few more probably come back full circle rather than entertain new cycles." She waits a second. "Is that how it feels, being here now?"

"'Full circle' you mean?" Owen imagines her nodding. "No. It's meant to be a goodbye, before I go off to start another chapter. Probably the last chapter."

It is the first time he has considered the future in such terms. For Owen, his life had been a series small leaps from one thing to the next. Sometimes these had been driven by the women coming into and then going out of his life; sometimes they had been engineered by work, location. He wonders how many times he had actually made a definitive choice himself — and now here was Maddie demanding to know 'what next?'

"You might be getting closer," she says cryptically.

"To what?"

His question is met with soft laughter. Owen had always hated it when she had the answer to a question but refused to tell him what it was.

XIV

Having just finished packing in readiness for his return to London, Owen had been standing at the top of the stairs looking down. Getting ready to leave was always a short and somewhat dissatisfying ritual, although he could never really establish why. With work being unusually challenging, taking an extra day to make a long weekend away had proved an inspired decision. If Maddie's fleeting presence had been an unexpected bonus, he was nonetheless convinced that in terms of unwinding from everyday stresses he had managed to use the time in Alma Road more successfully than his sister. Her voice — and that of Florence — floated up from the hall towards him, an incursion of sufficient interest to arrest his progress with his re-packed case and leave him leaning against the balustrade at the top of the stairs. From his vantage point he could make out a vertical slice of Maddie, one foot on the bottom step, her body turned to face the kitchen door where he was sure his aunt was standing.

"I do admire your resilience," Florence was saying.

"Is that what you think it is?" Maddie replied. "Not stupidity or bloodymindedness?"

Florence laughed a little.

"Well, perhaps with a touch of those mixed in too." When the slightest of pauses looked likely to trigger Maddie's resumption of her stair climb, Florence pushed on. "It must be difficult," she suggested.

"What?"

"To put disappointment behind you and move on — and with apparent ease — as if it didn't matter."

"Ah." Maddie turned her body sufficiently to allow her to sit on the third step, her head still inclined towards the kitchen. "Well, in the first instance it does matter, and in the second it isn't easy — even if you think I strive to make it seem so. It's always hard being told that your work isn't good enough. But it goes with the territory; you have to take it on the chin. After a while — after all this time — in theory it gets easier, but it never gets 'easy'." Maddie paused to consider the second part of Florence's statement. "And as for moving on, what else are you supposed to do? If you didn't, you'd only paint one picture in your entire life because when it was turned down you couldn't possibly paint another." She laughed, though without conviction. "I confess I have felt like that on more than one occasion. Giving up, I mean."

From his perch high above them Owen could tell Maddie was only partly joking. They had spoken often enough about her difficulties in placing and selling work for him to know that whatever brave face she had chosen to put on, the process ground her down from time to time. Perhaps increasingly so. He didn't think he had ever seen her as fragile as he had that weekend.

"Of course, you do have one advantage over everyone else," Florence offered in response.

"What's that?"

"Your brilliance."

Maddie laughed at the semi-joke, throwing back her head a little as she did so. For a split second Owen was worried that he might be discovered eavesdropping.

"You're right," Maddie said, making the effort to stand up again. "I always have that to fall back on; the knowledge that one day some curator or gallery owner will recognise my true worth and then suddenly everything will be different. People will look back at all my earlier work and say 'how did we miss *her*?' It's only a matter of time."

A final unheard word from Florence brought the exchange to an end. Owen pushed himself back from the banister towards his door and then, just as Maddie reached the half-landing, made out he was emerging from his room.

"Alright, Sis?"

"Never better."

And she breezed past him and into her room.

"I knew you were there, you know." Present day Maddie putting the record straight.

"You did not."

She laughs.

"Of course I did. When I leant back to laugh at that thing Florence said about my brilliance, you were there in my peripheral vision. There's always something or someone in the corner of your eye. Have you ever noticed that?"

"I've no idea what you're talking about."

"Ah well, I suppose that's the beauty and the curse of being brilliant."

Her voice seems to be coming from below him, and Owen imagines her once again sitting on that third step — only this time looking up at him. The fancy makes him smile.

"If you like," she says.

"What?"

"I'll sit here, on this step, and talk to you. If it helps. Seems fitting anyway."

"How 'fitting'?"

"Because it ties together that little incident you just remembered with where you are now, physically; with you there and me here; one of us looking up, the other one down. A kind of fusion of past and present, don't you think?"

"Can you do that with time?" he asks, as much to himself as to her. And yet it seems as if he has proved you can. In these last few seconds he has stood still yet traversed the years. He is a different person today, of course; older and hopefully wiser than he had been, what, twenty years earlier. And Maddie is... Well, one way or another she is still Maddie.

"The house is the constant," she suggests. "These rooms, that banister rail, this step. Though I have to say that the carpet is looking a little threadbare, so could probably do with a refresh; as could the paintwork."

"Jobs for the new owners then." Expecting some kind of comeback, Owen senses her deliberately ignore his comment. "You know I never really understood all that stuff about brilliance."

"I know." There is an air of tolerance in her voice, and in it Owen is sure he can hear echoes of Florence. "And I know it didn't matter to you."

He accepts the challenge.

"I wouldn't say it didn't matter. Of course it mattered. Perhaps it was just that I had difficulty relating to the notion; after all, I could never really tell a good painting from a bad one. I had to rely on other people for that kind of insight."

"You do yourself a disservice. And in any case, I didn't mean brilliance per se but rather my belief in my own, however shaky that became."

"But it wasn't just you," he corrects her. "Florence was your biggest fan remember." Spoken or not, the walls absorb the words, process them, add another layer to the lamination they have been building for the past fifty years. "Maybe it was the faith you had in yourself that I could never understand — faith never being my strong suit."

"As aunt pointed out on more than one occasion."

He laughs, remembering how recalcitrant he had been when it came to belief of any kind.

"But to me it seemed unshakeable, this certainty you possessed. Even in the darker times." It is statement which, having been made, potentially opens doors Owen prefer remained closed; doors which are not physical ones with handles and catches, yet somehow doors belonging to the house all the same. He looks around as if to count the rooms standing open about him, almost as if their present conversation might have succeeded in spawning another one behind his back. "If you think it didn't matter to me then that was only because I needed no additional attributes, no extraneous considerations, to make you any more significant to me than you already were."

He is unsure whether in making this denial — or affirmation — he has been able to convey a positive sense of what did 'matter'. It was like meaning taken from a photographic negative; the reverse is what is important. Nor does he have any inkling as to how Maddie might have taken such a declaration — either then or now.

"You were always too pragmatic for such fanciful things as brilliance, weren't you Glen? Real or imagined. You'd take the monotone and concrete over the nebulous any day of the week."

"And is there anything wrong with that? It's not something I feel I need to apologise for."

"I'm not saying you do."

"Well then." Yet he is unable to leave it there, feeling he has not yet justified himself. "It is what it is; I suppose that's the way I think about life. What's the point of upsetting yourself with things that are outside of your control?" Aware this sounds like a direct criticism of her and how she came to lead her life, he volunteers for another bullet. "And before you say anything, yes I do include Wendy and Lisa and Grace in that. Other men, more 'romantic' men, men who 'believed' in things might have gone to pieces when such women left them; but I didn't. Dusted myself down..."

"So what are you doing now?" Maddie stops him short.

"Now?"

"Standing at the top of the stairs talking to an empty house. Surely that demonstrates you appreciate something beyond 'it is what it is'? Or beyond what you can only see and touch? Or are you making an exception on my account?"

"I'll always make an exception on your account," he says, ducking the segue into the metaphysical. "I'm only saying that I didn't need you to be brilliant for you to be the sister I loved. And that I struggled with the concept irrespective of that."

Owen waits for Maddie to respond. As he does so, he scans the stairwell again, noticing not only the large ghosted space where her tall Pre-Raphaelite had hung, but smaller rectangles ascending the walls on either side. He wonders whether it would be possible for different pictures to hang in those spaces and prove as suitable as the originals; or whether they would need to be at least the same size — if not larger — in order to disguise the boundaries between the light-worn wallpaper and where it had previously been protected. He thinks of the rusted iron railings — and then reminds himself how the stairwell might look in the future isn't his problem.

"That's nice of you," Maddie's voice again, "the sort of thing a sister needs to hear from her brother on occasion."

"Well. Of course. I'm just sorry if I didn't say it enough, that's all."

"It's okay. I knew anyway." A break while she shifts her train of thought. "And to be honest, there's a part of me that wishes I'd been more like you."

"Oh?"

"The 'it is what it is' part. Maybe it would have been better if I hadn't been so determined or so certain. Or increasingly concerned about being uncertain."

"About being brilliant?"

When Maddie fails to immediately answer, Owen attributes a nod of the head to her. It is enough.

"But I was. It was my defining characteristic in many ways; what drove me on, made me do some of the things I did that on reflection… Strange how that certainty seemed to change its composition over time even as, in reality, likelihood receded. I think it became more frantic somehow. You'd imagine that rejection after rejection — even with the odd success thrown in — would have beaten me down sooner than it did. It could hardly have impacted me any more than it did."

"Some people would have given up," he suggests, attempting to be soothing, "but you didn't. Isn't that worth something?"

"You tell me. And how do you measure that kind of worth anyway? For years I couldn't see that the horse I kept backing only had three legs. It was never going to win."

"You don't know that," Owen protested.

"Perhaps. Let's just say that it wasn't going to win in my lifetime. Is that any better? Can you suddenly expect it to come romping home in another lifetime given you're not there to ride it?"

As far as Owen could see it wasn't just that it didn't win, it didn't even finish the race.

"On reflection, I don't think Florence helped."

"My greatest advocate?" Maddie is clearly surprised.

"Would it have made a difference if she hadn't kept egging you on, trying to boost your confidence, telling you to get back in the saddle?"

"I'm not sure that's entirely fair."

"But you can answer the question — after all, you're the only one who can."

They had returned one year to celebrate George's seventieth birthday. Wendy had been on the scene for about a year. Owen, Maddie and Florence were standing outside in the garden in order to allow Maddie to smoke, a vice she adopted sporadically — usually when she was under stress. She had been telling them of a 'near miss' with a submission to a Manchester gallery.

"...but being on the shortlist isn't good enough. First loser doesn't pay the bills."

"Are things tight?" Florence had asked.

Maddie smiled.

"More or less hand-to-mouth, but not desperate."

"Next time, dear. It only takes one enlightened person." Florence put her hand on Maddie's arm, shot Owen a knowing glance. "What's next? You must have something else in the pipeline."

"The pipeline isn't the problem, aunt; it's squeezing something through it and out the other end that's difficult."

"London again?" Owen tried to be encouraging, but based on Florence's expression knew he had fallen short.

"I expect so. Frank's down there at the moment trying to wangle us an invitation to submit to a show that opens in

Lewisham in a few weeks. He's good at that. And it's half the battle, getting your foot in the door. He's my PR man."

"And is he any good at it?" It was the logical question, but once it was out Owen knew he could have phrased it better. At that moment he wished Wendy had been out in the garden with them; she would have rescued him.

"He is actually. Quite the charmer."

Owen had met Frank once; his assessment had been entirely different. He'd described him to Wendy as "a slimy individual; I wouldn't trust him as far as I could throw him". It was partly that assessment which made him certain that — like most of Maddie's boyfriends — Frank was destined to occupy the role only on a temporary basis.

"So that's the easy part," Maddie continued. "Then it's down to me and my brilliance." She offered a short chuckle. "Thinking about it, I might submit the piece I sent to Manchester; and that abstract still life I did for the Chester thing last year. Do you remember the one?"

"I do," Florence slipped into over-supportive mode, "so vibrant. They're bound to love it. Don't you think, Owen?"

As if knowing Owen can't possibly have remembered it, the contemporary Maddie can't help but break in to her brother's recollection.

"And did you?"

"Did I what?"

"Remember it? Think it was any good? 'Love it', even?"

There were so many paintings, was it forgivable for him to not recall them all? He looks at the large un-discoloured rectangle of wallpaper in front of him as if he might find a clue there. From somewhere in his brain two synapses spark.

"Was it a bottle and two oranges — but distorted in such a way that you almost couldn't tell which was which?"

He hears a whistle emanating from where he imagines Maddie sitting. She rarely whistled.

"Go to the top of the class, brother mine. Perhaps today will be a day of surprises after all." He is unable to suppress a smile. "And do you remember what happened to it?"

Although she has attempted to keep her tone light, her voice still gives away the answer.

"I can guess."

"You see that space two down from the half-landing? Instead of being in Lewisham and selling for hundreds of pounds, it ended up there, in Florence's own private gallery."

"Perhaps she thought that to keep putting your pictures on the way was evidence enough. To keep you going, I mean. Something to shore-up your belief. Better on the wall here than sitting in a dusty pile in your flat."

Maddie says nothing, and Owen stares down at the third step as if doing so might permit her to materialise. But all he can see are the worn treads. He straightens and looks toward the bedroom their aunt and uncle had shared for over fifty years. What is to be gained by going in there? For a moment he fears he has let Maddie down; that in being inadequately complete or incomplete, in being so black-and-white ('it is what it is'), his memory has betrayed not only her but perhaps the house too. It is an odd notion, but a sufficiently strong one for him to wonder if he has already done enough damage to her — or the house has done enough damage to him.

"You need to keep plugging away." Maddie's voice, its location once again indeterminate.

"Like you did?"

"No, like you always did…"

XV

Walking through its door, his aunt and uncle's room is the last room in the house left to visit. Coincident with that recognition is the realisation that it is also the room he knows least well, inevitably so given how infrequently he and Maddie were permitted to cross its threshold. Even though this is the case, his memory of it is oddly sharp, perhaps as a result of the monumental furniture Florence and George used to prefer: the large bed, the huge wardrobe in the far corner, the twin sets of drawers either side of a small vanity table. His and hers. And all in oak. No longer obscured by their chattels, the wallpaper on one of the walls — a vivid pattern involving birds-of-paradise and vines — now seems incongruous. If he can still make out the room's distinct aroma, he is reminded that he had never liked it. Lily-of-the-valley perhaps — or was that merely a default male answer when a fragrance was unknown? Yet it had always been there, this benign smell, presumably soaking itself into the fabric of the walls. The new owners would need to do more than simply open windows to rid themselves of it — which would, he decides, be something of a shame. To erase the smell entirely might be to take the last of Florence and George out of the place.

In as much as someone might turn over the borders and plant them to a new design, or redecorate the stairwell to remove those rectangular traces of Maddie, so Owen was beginning to feel as if the house — as he had known and loved it — was on borrowed time. If in three or four years he found himself once again standing on the pavement looking over the wall, would it be the new things upon which he would first alight or the absence of the old? Removal of the railings' rust and their subsequent re-painting would be entirely insignificant, but if the hebe was gone or the arch through the hedge had been butchered or chunks of the lawn turned to gravel, what would that tell him? He tries to picture such a scene and is unable to reconcile it with the fact that he would be standing on the same tree-lined street and be looking at number seventeen. Perhaps under cover of darkness the new owners might have swapped it with number twenty one, the only other house on the road he regarded as remotely similar, for how could this house — their house — be anything other than what it has always been?

"Strange how you can get attached to things," Maddie says. Perhaps she is over by the window looking down into the front garden. "I mean, it's only bricks and mortar, wallpaper and carpets, hedges and flowers."

"Or unattached," Owen suggests.

"Don't tell me you don't care for the place any more."

"No, not that. You misunderstand. I was thinking about how easy it can be to disassociate yourself from things; people mostly. How, after a relatively short period of time, it's almost as if they were never there."

"I hope that's not aimed in my direction." She laughs.

"Never," he says, knowing all too well that Maddie accepts he is beyond such callousness. Isn't he proving it at this precise moment? "No, I was thinking about other people. And before you accuse me of it, no-one who has ever lived this house."

"It gets in your bones," she offers — which seems a strange assertion, considering.

"Or even *is* your bones. In a way." Owen wonders about the origin of the metaphor. "If bones are what give you shape and keep you from falling into a heap, then didn't this house do that for us?"

In the pause which follows he goes to where the wardrobe stood and runs his fingers over the wall.

"That's unusually non-literal. And perceptive too."

"You approve then?"

"How could I not?"

He walks to the window imagining Maddie making way for him — but just in case she doesn't give ground entirely, confines himself to its right-hand side.

"I think I spent more time in here after George died than in all those years we lived here before. What about you?"

"If you recall I wasn't around that much after uncle died. I was away wrestling demons…"

"Yes. Sorry." He turns away from the view as if he just seen something he would rather have not, trailing his eyes around the picture rail as a distraction.

"And why was that?" Maddie asked. "I mean, why in here so much?"

"Oh, mainly to help Florence sort a few things out. She did very little of that immediately after George died, and then just as she was working up to it — well, you took our minds off of just about everything else… So perhaps it would have been late 2018, something like that. She'd sift through drawers and we'd talk. Sometimes I'd be the one doing the sifting and she would just sit on the bed and pass judgement."

"Judgement?"

"On what to do with George's old clothes. Not that there was very much to decide: which charity shop they should go to, things like that. In the end I don't think she kept very much."

"And did you do the same with my things?"

It is a question he had not seen coming, but his answer is ready enough.

"I kept everything. When I cleared the house I put the contents of your room into three or four large boxes. They're in storage. I didn't have the strength to go through them."

"Scaredy-cat." Maddie laughs. Owen knows she doesn't mean it. "I do remember one conversation though."

"Oh?"

"The three of us, soon after he died. She was worried that she'd pushed him too hard."

"That was in here?" Owen struggles to physically locate the conversation.

"I'm not sure. Probably not. But it was definitely the three of us."

Owen propels himself back into the kitchen (the most likely setting) the three of them sat around the table, coffee steaming from mugs.

"You know," Florence said, looking not at them but toward the window and the garden outside, the tone of her voice betraying the fact that she knew she would never see George through that window again, "I sometimes wonder if I was a little hard on your uncle."

"Hard? How so?" Almost inevitably it was Maddie seeking clarification.

"Pushing him." Florence saw a flicker of misunderstanding cross his niece's face. "Mainly in the invisible things, you understand. I was never one of those shouty domineering wives, screaming all the time."

"I think we'd struggle to see you in that role," Owen confirmed. They laughed. "But 'invisible'?"

Florence looked at them in turn.

"Should I expect you to understand? Oh, I know you've had your relationships, your ups and downs, and that you'll run them in the way to suit you." Not aiming to be judgemental, she paused to allow either of them to interject, to defend themselves. "But it's different when you're married. At least that's what I think. There's a certain permanence about it."

"No backing out?" Maddie suggested.

"Aren't you youngsters always prepared to find a way out?" Although a joke, Florence was immediately concerned that she may have gone too far. She placed a hand on Maddie's arm. "Lots of people think marriage makes no difference, is out-dated, just an excuse for a party. But it was never that for me."

"Nor George," Owen suggested.

"Indeed," Florence paused, "even though he ended up with me."

They laughed again.

"But wasn't he happy?" Maddie asked. "He always seemed happy to us, didn't he, Glen? You both did."

"Oh, we were, we were. But you have to work at it. Always."

"So how were you hard on him?" Owen brought them back to Florence's statement.

Florence smiled, then looked again towards the window.

"I set the bar high, I think. What I expected my life to look like. Not emotionally — we were always devoted I think — but practically." She looked up and around the kitchen, and then frowned slightly as if trying to see through the walls. "This place. Although there were elements that were his — we divided the house up in a way — I think I made my expectations for all of it very clear."

"Like the garden?" Maddie suggested.

"The garden?" Florence weighed up the notion. "Perhaps at first — but the garden was never an issue. His first love in many respects."

"That I doubt." Maddie brought a smile and a nod from her aunt.

"But there were things I wanted. This room decorated, that room re-carpeted. Although I knew we would grow old together with the house, I didn't want the house to grow old at the same rate, to feel stale. Do you know what I mean? Of course you two helped make the place come alive, but I always felt it should regenerate itself, gradually, over time." She paused again. "You wouldn't have seen any of that. The outcome of it, perhaps, but not the discussions that drove them on. Or drove him on."

Getting a glimpse of where Florence had been heading, Owen settled on the crux of it.

"And you're worried that may have contributed to his illness?"

Florence nodded.

Maddie stood and walked round to where her aunt sat and wrapped her arms about her, hoping doing so would have been sufficient to reassure her — just as such gestures were intended to work on her.

"Do you think she believed us, Glen?" Maddie asks.

"Probably not. You know Florence: once she had an idea in her head it was often difficult to shift." He thinks back to some of the things she had said about Grace, Lisa and Wendy. "If not impossible."

"And George?"

"What about him?"

"Do you think he was aware of her concern that she was somehow culpable for his decline, even in a small way?"

It is not a suspicion he is conscious of ever having; and yet as he scans his memory to see if he can settle on the extent of Florence's responsibility toward George — indeed, the kind of interaction he might have ended up experiencing with Wendy — he cannot help but conjure unbidden an image of Maddie, the Maddie who is speaking to him now. He tries to beat away the question that is building, to drag them back.

"I can't see it. And anyway wasn't what she ended up feeling the sort of guilt people inevitably suffer after losing a loved one?"

"Is it?"

Owen lets it go.

"Of course we didn't see what aunt saw. We grew up with the garden always immaculate and assumed that was all because of uncle. And it probably was. But as for the house? If you think about it, every year there was something new: a room being decorated, or a new carpet, or some new furniture."

"Maybe all of it combined to make us believe that was just how life was lived." Owen nods in response. Maddie pushes on. "But if so, I feel sorry for the house."

Her statement throws him.

"How so?"

"Because it has been unchanged and unloved for nearly four years now. Abandoned."

"You talk as if it was sentient, a person." He allows a gap for Maddie to interject. Silence. Is it possible that there is a link between Alma Road and this incarnation of Maddie? Is he talking to the house as much as he is talking to her — if indeed he is talking to anyone at all? Either way, he feels compelled to respond. "I can't disagree. But for her to think she pushed him over the edge somehow... Ridiculous, really."

Moving away from the wall, Owen walks slowly to the door. And yet something tells him that he is far from done.

"But that's not all, is it?"

It almost feels as if Maddie is now on his shoulder, her question whispered, certain of the answer even before he gives it.

"What do you mean?"

"There's more to tell about Florence and George."

"You mean secrets?" Having said it, Owen smiles nervously at the word. He wonders if he has opened the door to a cupboard beyond which all the unspoken things lurk, those truths to which the house has clung over the years. Perhaps he opened that door — or all those doors — as soon as he turned the key in the lock beneath the tarnished number seventeen. If so, then surely what lies beyond can only be benevolent given he has always assumed that stashing away of some truths was driven more by a desire to protect than from any devious malevolence.

"If you like."

The tone of her voice, seemingly suggesting Owen has a choice, delivers the words in such a way as to affirm that he has none.

"I'm not sure I've ever liked secrets," Owen says, stalling.

"We all have them," Maddie says. "Some more than others. Even Florence."

And although he believes his aunt would have been the last person in the world to harbour secrets, he knows that she did — because she shared them with him. If he is aware of that, then surely his present-day Maddie must be too.

Owen walks to where one of the chests of drawers once stood, placing himself as close to where he had been standing that day as if doing so will ease the passage of memory. He had been holding a grey cable-knit jumper in his right hand.

"There was someone else you know."

As if it possessed a force all its own, Florence's voice had made him turn. It was a statement devoid of any anchor in time.

"Someone else?"

From the look on his face, Florence immediately saw Owen trying to join dots.

"Before we were married, I mean." She chuckled — though whether at the memory she was resurrecting or Owen's reaction to her words he was unable to say. "He was called Charlie. The same age as me, so younger than your uncle. We went to school together. We were what might, in common parlance, be called 'childhood sweethearts'."

Unsure how to respond, Owen waited for Florence to unravel a little more of the story.

"I think as I grew older, through my teenage years, I had a growing sense of — I don't know — what you might call 'destiny'. It seemed inevitable that Charlie and I would end up together."

"And why didn't you?"

"Oh, that's easy." Florence watched as Owen laid the grey jumper on the bed, using those few moments to recompile her story. "In the first instance because of your father. Augustus was younger than me and therefore younger than Charlie, but he'd never liked Charlie, always played up when he was around. I think he was trying to frighten him off — which obviously didn't go down too well with me. I could see Charlie wondering what life would be like with Augustus as a brother-in-law. And maybe he also came to wonder whether I might have had ended up displaying similarly unpleasant traits; peas from the same pod, and all that."

"But surely he knew you well enough?"

"I liked to think so." Florence allowed herself a moment to chase the image of Augustus away. "And the second reason I didn't marry Charlie was because of your uncle. When I met him, well… He was older than Charlie, and I hadn't really met any young men of your uncle's age so hadn't appreciated the difference a few years could make. On that basis, George was a different kettle of fish altogether. And because he was that little bit older I already had an insight into what sort of a mature man he would make. I had no clue about Charlie, not really. So much can change you in your early twenties…"

"Was that the fundamental attraction, uncle being more mature?"

"Only in part. What seemed to matter more was that I thought your uncle needed me. I had this wild notion that he required rescuing somehow, and that I was just the girl to do it. So I did. Or at least I tried to."

Leaving the jumper on the bed, Owen rose and walked back to the set of drawers. From the bottom one he removed another and turned to face Florence intending to ask her what she wanted to do with it — only to find her cradling the sweater he had just deposited alongside her.

"And did you rescue him?"

Florence smiled.

"What do you think? You're probably a better judge of that than I could ever be."

"Well," Owen pretended to give the matter some thought, "I can't say uncle ever struck me as someone who needed saving, therefore you must have achieved that before we came along."

She laughed gently.

"I suspect we'd rescued each other by then. And continued to do so — especially when having you and Maddie here with us was so new and initially so difficult."

"But you rescued us too," Owen said, "and in a very real way. I think you deserved a medal, both of you."

"Oh we had our rewards right enough."

He placed the newly extracted jumper on the bed; Florence deposited the grey one on on top of it.

"Did you ever think about Charlie?"

"And wonder what life with him would have been like? I used to, for a little while. Even though I think he was heart-broken, I kept in touch with him for a short while; and then he went off to Canada and that was that." She looked at both jumpers, then back to Owen, a frown building on her face. "I don't want you to think I ever had any regrets about your uncle. There were none. It was the right choice; we fitted each other. If there are any regrets then they certainly aren't related to my choosing him over Charlie."

Feeling their purpose had been somewhat derailed, all Owen could do was pull another sweater from the drawer, the last one; it was a shade of green Maddie had always liked and Florence hated, and for that reason it had been relegated to the status of one of George's 'gardening jumpers'.

"What was he like when you met him?"

"Your uncle?"

Owen nodded, then moved towards Florence whose arms were already out to receive the final garment which she took from him with surprising gentleness. Although he knew the story of their meeting, he wondered if there might be something cathartic in giving her the opportunity to replay it once again, now that he was gone. Sitting back on the bed, the sweaters resting there stood guard between the two of them.

"He had a difficult childhood, I think." Florence began is if she was answering a different question — or because she knew there was a precursor Owen hadn't considered. "There was the war of course; he was eight when it started, but he told you that didn't he? I think in many ways he was protected from it as much as he could have been. As much as they tried to protect all children, I suppose. But where there had been just Augustus and me, George had been the youngest of five: two older brothers and two older sisters. You knew that too, didn't you?" Florence paused, realising that she needed to fill the gap she had just created. "I never met any of them. Sam and William had been old enough to fight. Sam joined the Air Force in thirty-eight I think it was, and William the navy in nineteen-forty. For a long while it looked as if they were both going to make it through unscathed but in the space of a few weeks in early forty-four Sam was shot down over Holland and William's ship struck a mine somewhere in the Mediterranean. Your uncle didn't say, but I think he'd been most fond of William, which made his death hardest to take — especially as it seemed it had just been the result of bad luck."

"He never really talked about them in any great detail."

"No, he didn't. And rarely to me. He once confessed to being desperate to fight as a result of their deaths — but what could a fourteen-year-old do when it was all over?" Although rhetorical, Florence made a show of waiting for an answer.

"And the girls?" Even though he had a sketch of their background, Owen offered up another question; Florence's perspective seemed suddenly important in order to apply rounded edges to their story.

"Peggy and Marge were born between William and George. When the war finished they were just getting started; Peggy was nineteen and Marge eighteen. I'm not sure George was ever that fond of them — not that he would ever have admitted such a thing. From what I understand I don't think he was like them at all, so maybe that's where that dislike came from."

"In what way?"

Florence ran a hand along the surface of the jumper she was holding then added it to the pile.

"By all accounts it seems as if they regarded the end of the war as an opportunity to break free. And let's be fair, they would have had a hard time of it too." She stood and then went to the chest of drawers. "Not all the American soldiers went home straight away, and Peggy and Marge managed to snare one each. The way he told me the story, theirs seemed a mercenary premeditated kind of enterprise. By forty-seven they were both living in the States, relatively remote places somewhere in the middle of nowhere. Your uncle never saw them again."

The notion struck Owen as absurd.

"But why ever not? Transatlantic travel was soon to become relatively easy wasn't it? There'd be no reason for George not to go and visit, or for them to come home."

"You would think so, wouldn't you?" Florence looked into the empty bottom drawer and bending, pushed it closed. Then she stood and turned to face into the room. "So in a relatively short period of time he had gone from being one-of-five to being one-of-one. The war taking all his siblings from him had shaped him, how could it not? We were all shaped by it; and not just the war itself, but the difficult years immediately afterwards. Some young people — those who had been hardened by their experiences I suppose — coped better than others. Your uncle struggled with it all, which is why he would never have spoken of it, not really. I think there was a post-war 'sink or swim' mentality in the late forties and early fifties, and you were either made that way or your weren't. George wasn't — though that of course made his move into academia all the more comforting. His university life, his world of research and study, papers and lectures, offered him a degree of insulation to protect him from what was going on outside. He didn't exactly withdraw because he'd never really 'come out', if you see what I mean. He found a way to protect himself from it. I don't think he was ever that good with things he didn't adequately understand. Perhaps he reinvented some of his past in order to make it more palatable. I think he died thinking he loved his sisters — and that he always had. I wasn't so sure."

Owen watched his aunt as she turned toward the window, looked out onto the street beyond. He tried to imagine what she saw, what she had seen.

"I understand what you mean when you said you thought he needed to be rescued."

"Do you, dear?" Her voice came to him from over her shoulder. "Well then."

Although she was standing just a few feet from him, Owen felt the distance between them expand, as if time could do that, manipulate the physics of things. Science hadn't been George's field, but Owen found himself wondering whether he might have found a theory to explain such things nevertheless.

"And you?" he asked.

"Me what?" Florence turned. Owen thought he caught the trace of a tear in her eye.

"Did you cope? Did Augustus?"

She laughed.

"Augustus coped soon enough." It was a phrase delivered in the certain knowledge that more might follow it should she choose to go down that path. She did not. "Our history was very different to your uncle's. We didn't lose anyone to the war for a start. Oh, my mother and father did their bit at home, in the factories and government offices, but they were never combative people. Quaker stock, you see. Lapsed Quakers maybe, but there are elements of such an upbringing, such a history, that probably takes a generation or more to leak away. Personally, I remember very little of the war. I was doing all my growing up in its aftermath, trying to carve out a place for myself in a country that was striving to establish itself in the new order. Everyone was really. There was little remarkable about me compared to your uncle."

Now it became Owen's turn to smile.

"You'll forgive me if I beg to differ."

"In what way?" It was a genuine enquiry, not an attempt to garner flattery.

"There is so much that is remarkable about you aunt," Owen said, then struggled to land on a suitable example. "Your ability to rescue people," was what he settled on.

"In the end we were middle class I suppose." It was a statement delivered from something of a tangent, as if it might have helped explain everything. "We didn't suffer in the same way most people did; there was little depravation in our family. And we had a safety net."

It was a phrase which could only pique Owen's interest.

"'Safety net'?"

"Money; here and there. Augustus and I had one uncle, Duncan, who'd made a small fortune in linoleum as the country came out of the Depression. An unmarried man, he'd always been very generous: helped Augustus and Alice when they married; gave me a tidy sum when it came to buying this place." Florence stopped and glanced around the room, examining the walls, seemingly wanting to satisfy herself that they were still in place.

"The house is yours?"

Florence looked at him as if the question had been uttered in a language with which she was only partially familiar.

"It was always *ours;* mine and George's. And then yours too, of course." And here she tried to undermine the language in which Owen had posed his question. "I have never wanted to think about the house from a purely financial perspective. Never."

XVI

As he walks back down the stairs, Owen wonders if, in the intervening years since his aunt's death, the house has ever felt like his, something he owned — and concludes it hasn't. No matter what the lawyers tell him or the legal papers say, surely it will always belong to Florence and George. He can't help but wonder what she might have said had he been able to confront her right here and now with that very same question about ownership, ask her to apply it to the place on this precise day. Unsurprisingly he can envisage two answers: the first is that the house always seemed to own itself, that they were merely custodians, and that it will always be so. And the second? It is the second answer — most likely entangled with duty and legacy — which concerns him. It is not fear of ownership nor lack of willpower or uncertainty which assails him, nor is it the complete opposite; rather, it is something he is unable to name. Perhaps it is a word from a lexicon with which — in one way or another — he at least seems to have so much trouble.

This notion of parallel languages comes to him much in the same way as the notion of parallel worlds and the liminal spaces between them which are inhabited by — who knows what? And even if theories of a 'multiverse' are no more than superstitious claptrap, he is forced to engage with it because of Maddie — not simply as a younger sister who seemed to live her life in a world at odds with his own, a world where their realms collided only so often (and always in Alma Road), but also because of her presence here, today, whispering in his ear, as if she has once again broken through from wherever she may be now, reawakened in the nebulous form she has chosen to take.

And then the idea strikes him that perhaps it is he and not Maddie who is the interloper; that when he pushed open the rusted gate, crossed the threshold, *he* was the one who was breaking through boundaries, leaving behind the world in which he was most comfortable and transgressing into another. Into hers. Or into the house's. Or even both.

And inevitably into another time too.

Pausing at the bottom of the stairs, he realises he needs to urinate and so slips into the downstairs loo. "There was another door after all" he says to himself, as if it were a private joke. The black-and-white floor tiles and white walls are familiar of course, and he has probably been in many similar bathrooms over the years. Bathrooms are not special; there is no reason to feel attachment here. He rinses his hands and then, in the absence of a towel, shakes them vigorously, all the while staring into the face that greets him in the mirror. It is then he sees it, hanging on the wall behind the door, a solitary little pen-and-ink sketch the removal men must have missed.

This one he remembers.

They had gone to the coast at one point during the summer immediately following his A-levels and before he headed off to university. After a while camped on the beach, he and George had gone off in search of ice creams leaving Florence and Maddie behind. When they returned, his aunt was looking out to sea, his sister sketching the coast in the opposite direction. Although unchanged, the distance between them seemed immeasurably large.

"And you're wondering if you missed something?" Maddie's voice emanates from somewhere close enough to make him blush.

"Is nothing sacred?"

Owen lifts the picture from the simple pin upon which it is hung and carries it with him from the lavatory and back into the hallway. Neither trophy nor souvenir, he is unable to decide what it might represent — if anything at all.

"Well you didn't." Chastened or not, his sister is back. "Miss anything I mean. We had been talking about my A-levels and how important they were, and what I might do at university, and then what I might do after that. It was no more secretive than that."

"I didn't say it was secretive," he protests.

"Oh, sorry; I thought that's where we'd got to, revealing secrets." Maddie allows a small but pointed gap. "It didn't strike me at the time how much of our lives aunt had planned out for us."

"Why do you say that?"

"That afternoon — while you were off getting the mint-choc-chip or whatever it was — it was evident that she had been thinking about it a great deal. Didn't you ever get that sense?"

Owen moves the sketch to his left hand and heads for the back door, his right hand playing with the keys in his pocket once again. Apart from general academia-related conversations with both she and George, he is unable to recollect any such plan relating to himself.

"Perhaps I didn't matter so much," he suggests, though without any bitterness, "because unlike you I was never going to do anything extraordinary. And by the way, it wasn't mint-choc-chip. None of us liked the stuff."

Maddie laughs.

"The things you remember."

"And the things I forget," he offers, pulling the back door open and moving into the garden once again.

It is as it was before he entered the house although with the sun a fraction lower the shapes and lengths of the shadows have changed, and the whole feels more muted than before. Returning to the bench, he sits. Looking along the borders he half-expects something magical to have happened while he was wandering around inside the house, that Maddie might have had once more surprise for him in this strange place where worlds and time seemed to collide, reverberate, imitate each other. He had forgotten the pen-and-ink until he had seen it hanging on the toilet wall. That afternoon he and George had bought strawberry for Maddie, vanilla for Florence, and chocolate for the two of them. Once again Maddie was right: the things he remembered.

He rests the beach sketch in his lap.

"And did I, Glen?"

It is as if her drawing is speaking to him.

"Did you do what?" he asks the sketch.

"Something extraordinary."

How does he quantify that? He looks down at the drawing again and knows he could never have achieved anything so subtle, so beautiful. Indeed, he would never have attempted it in the first place. Is that enough? Or did the drawing need to be more than depict accuracy, beauty? It was authentic. It looked like the place they had visited. Yet he is naggingly aware that when one is thinking in terms of being 'extraordinary', faithful depiction is largely redundant. Is the greater significance that the drawing triggered memory or emotion? If so, how might its ability to do so fare as measure of the extraordinary? Owen wants to qualify it in — if only to make his task easier — but instinctively knows he cannot. Arriving at such a position informs him that personal attachment disqualifies him as a judge, and if that is the case how can he possibly answer Maddie's question? But she has asked him and he feels obliged to give her an answer.

"Not even Parliament takes this long," Maddie chides playfully.

There is only one answer he wants to be able to give her — 'yes' — but he needs to be able to support his assertion because he knows she will challenge it. Evidence is the thing. And then he wonders whether Maddie might have already settled on an outcome, and that this is more of a test for him than a measure of her.

"Extraordinary?" He buys just a little time. "Yes, of course." He waits for her voice, but having recognised the need for justification, knows Maddie will have seen that too. "It was evident all over this house," he offers.

"How so?"

"Because you helped make it beautiful. And because you made Florence happy. And proud. Is there anything more extraordinary than that?"

Weak argument or not, he chooses to let the notion stand on its own two feet while simultaneously wondering whether he had ever done anything even remotely important enough to make their aunt proud. Inevitably his conclusion is that there was nothing in the mundanity of his professional life from which she could possibly have gained any satisfaction when measured against the same scale. Yes, she had been pleased when he had done well, been promoted; but his achievements were insignificant compared to that for which Maddie was striving.

"George had been proud of both of us," Maddie says, as if bypassing a question, "though he didn't really understand what I was trying to do — which made your successes all the more important for him."

"You think so?"

When she says nothing, Owen inserts the words "I know so" into the conversation, in her voice, just to round out at least that part of it. The measure of her achievement still hangs over him however, inadequately addressed.

"I'm not the best judge." He comes clean.

"That's honest. And probably true. Bias can be a bastard can't it?" She lets the statement hang in the air for a moment. "Which means I too am not well-placed to offer an opinion."

"Because you're your own worst critic?"

"Or because I always needed an ego boost. Still do."

Owen contemplates her assertion and the premise behind it. While he understands how self-esteem would have been important for Maddie, he's confused as to how it could still be relevant in her now dislocated timeline. Having never considered such matters before, he wonders when self-worth ceases to be important. You get older, priorities change; if you once wanted to be a fast bowler for England, at some point that becomes an irrelevant ambition — either due to lack of skill in the first place, or an increase in age in the second. And so you put the goal aside, ideally replacing it with something else, something more realistic. Reasonably certain it might be possible to land on a few such examples from his own life (if of a decidedly lower calibre), he brushes them away, wanting to concentrate on Maddie, her brilliance, her desire to do extraordinary things. At what point did her ambition cease to be relevant? Having assumed he could put a precise day, time and hour on such matters — and for obvious reasons — he is suddenly not so sure. Is her brilliance, her self-esteem relevant still?

"It's always relevant," she says, her voice a little way from him as if she has been pacing the lawn just beyond the edge of the patio, "because you can be extraordinary at any moment in time. And at all moments in time. Did Van Gogh cease to be brilliant just because he died? In a way it's not about the person, it's about their work. When I ask if I did anything extraordinary I'm not talking about me so much but rather about what people can still see. Like that little sketch you're cradling in your lap."

He looks down at it. Fluent, accurate, successfully depicting a place, a mood — even a time — but extraordinary? He doubts it. But then how would it be possible for Maddie — or even Van Gogh for that matter — to be brilliant all the time?

"I went on a workshop once," she is sitting beside him again. He can feel her eyes on the drawing. "It was about creating abstract versions of the human form; life drawing with a twist. Not Picasso or anything like that, but something more contemporary. Closer to Bacon maybe." She pauses, unsure whether she has lost him already. Recognising artists' names thanks to the limited but informed exposure she had gifted him, Owen nods. "Who knows, maybe my attending that workshop was about me once again wanting to find a new style, a new phase, trying something different. There were so many such inflection points along the way — not that you would have seen most of them."

There is a fall in her voice. Owen senses Maddie would be unable to identify all such pivotal moments herself should someone challenge her to do so.

"Perhaps I saw some of the results," he suggests, trying to prove he was engaged. "New paintings hanging on the walls whenever I came back to visit."

"Indeed — though you probably looked but didn't see." There is a short hiatus. Before he has the opportunity to be upset, she carries on. "Which is fair enough, given that's how most people look at art. Superficially, I mean. It's not intended to be a criticism of you."

Owen smiles.

"Don't worry, I'm not offended."

He wants to reach out, to touch her on the arm, the shoulder; to reassure her, as much as reassure himself.

"Anyway, this workshop," she says, returning to her theme. "Don't ask me what I was expecting, I can't possibly remember. And in any event, I always used to go to those things more in hope than expectation."

"When was it?"

"About seven years ago or so."

Surprised it was so recent, in such close proximity to her death, Owen is unable to keep his feelings hidden.

"I know, right?" Maddie laughs, intercepting them. "Desperate to the end. Still searching for something magical, just as I had been when I left home. As I always had been really. I'm sure that must say something about me."

"A desire to improve, to always be willing to try new things, not being prepared to settle for where you were." In terms of an up-side, it is the best he can manage.

"You're very sweet." Owen feels that her acknowledgement somehow matches the banality of his observation — then she pushes on without missing a beat. "So, no expectations. Safer that way. And probably the benefit of wisdom gained from having been disappointed so many times."

"Abstract people was no better?"

She laughs at his terminology.

"Abstract people are fine — it's the real ones I have trouble with…" A pause. "Actually the workshop was pretty good, a few twists on familiar techniques maybe; one or two new ideas."

"So why mention it?"

"There was a girl on the course, just out of college, trying to make her way in the world exactly as I had been — what? — nearly thirty years earlier. Bright, idealistic, unscarred."

"As we all are at some point."

Maddie lets it go.

"The difference with her — she was called Eloise — was that she was supremely talented, gifted, natural. She picked up the ideas and theories from the tutor in an instant, and then — in what seemed just a few minutes — had transformed them into something else. While the rest of us were struggling to get to grips with concepts, new notions of composition and balance — you name it — she was on a different planet."

"Good then?" Owen can't help but notice how Maddie has refrained from using the word 'brilliant'.

"Just a bit."

"But aren't there always people like that? I mean, won't there always be?" Not entirely sure what he means — nor what he is trying to say — Owen flounders a little. It feels as if they might be edging towards dangerous territory. Maddie must have had a reason for mentioning the workshop, but he is unable to make the connection between it, today, the house. Other than via the link through the drawing in his hand.

"Of course. And I've seen plenty of them over the years. A few who are really good — and lots who aren't but think they are. It's pretty easy to differentiate between the two. You get plenty of practice."

"So?" Looking down at the sketch again, believing it holds the clue he has missed, he finds himself wanting to hear the punchline.

"Eloise was different."

"'Different'?"

"I'd never come across anyone quite like her. She made creating great work so easy. And so was pleasant with it; unassuming, not big-headed. I found myself hoping that there was something about her to dislike, as if that would allow me to disqualify her art. But there was nothing, Glen. Just this really nice person producing stuff I could only dream of."

Trying to conjure a picture of this mythical creature, Owen struggles. He has no difficulty thinking of a really nice person and can even imagine one or two people he has known who might fit the bill; but aligning them with a quality which, for him, tends to exist in words rather than in hard physical evidence, is a task which floors him. He glances again at the beach scene. If it had been drawn by Degas or Leonardo or the postman, would he have been able to tell the difference? Is there be something about it — intrinsic but invisible — that defies him? He cannot doubt it.

"But presumably not for the first time. I mean there must have been a few other people whose work you'd envied over the years. Isn't that the nature of the beast?"

Her laugh is only partially sympathetic.

"Of course you're not wrong; and believe me, in Eloise's case I tried to do just that, to simply be envious. I really did. But I think there was something about being in the same place as her, watching the magic happen in 'real time'... There I was, nearly fifty years old, and I suddenly realised that I'd never had an experience like it."

Owen wants to suggest that watching Eloise work could have been inspiring, might have acted as a catalyst or encouraged Maddie to redouble her efforts; but there is something in her tone which prevents him from doing so. It is a warning that he would be wide of the mark.

Having reached this conclusion he knows he needs to say nothing; so he waits.

"One of the things I'd always assumed — clung to, if you like, a bit like a life-raft after a ship sinks — was that time and experience would add to my stock of skill and wisdom, and then transfer itself into tangible improvements in more work. And actually I like to think that it did. If I look back at my work as a twenty-, thirty-, forty-year-old you can see the progression. Even *you* could see the progression." It is a cheap but feeble joke delivered for neither of their benefits. "But watching Eloise I realised that I could live to be two-hundred and never scratch the surface of what she was already capable of."

"Isn't that all about perspective?" He is unsure if perspective is the correct term, or even a word he should be allowed to use; but he wants to suggest something about the relationship between the intangible concepts with which he is struggling. "After all, you could look at Gainsborough or Turner and still admire them even knowing you were never going to be in their league."

"Gainsborough? His would be a 'league' I wouldn't want be in. As for Turner, well..." She seems to make a show of thinking about it. "You're right, of course, but you miss the critical point. Eloise was alive, a contemporary of sorts. And I had been a witness."

Her last word strikes Owen as strange, almost religious in its overtones. Was it possible that what she had seen had been — for her — the equivalent of a miracle? It certainly sounded like it. And if so, how would that affect someone who had ambitions to work miracles of their own?

"It forced me — that workshop, Eloise — to look both back and forward: back to my baby-steps' progression and lack of producing anything seismic, and forward to a future where I could see..." She hesitates.

"What?"

"Nothing but more of the same. Eloise personified what it was I wanted — and what it was I could never have. She made me want to give up, there and then. Never lift another paint brush."

"But you did?"

"Because I managed to get over it? Or because I couldn't see any alternative?" The questions are clearly rhetorical, and Owen knows only one of them can be answered in the affirmative. "It's funny how, when it comes down to it, life is really just a long succession of binary decisions."

"You believe that?"

Not getting any answer, Owen gets the distinct impression that she has moved away from him; away, but not left him entirely. He stands, looks over his shoulder back to the house, then begins another circuit of the garden, this time anti-clockwise.

Perhaps it is as a direct result of his conversation with Maddie that his eyes are more attuned to the slight tonal differences in colour compared to when he had arrived, the result of a fading sun, the change in the angle of light. He allows himself a smile, the thought coming to him that she is still able to teach him things — open his eyes — after all this time. Doesn't that qualify as a brilliance of sorts, even if one were unable to justify or quantify it? Or sell it? Isn't there something unique about individuals who are still able to reach you long after they have gone? In his mind he replays his arguments about Van Gogh and Turner, and wonders whether they support him or not; then he pauses to turn and look back at the house and thinks of Florence and George. Are they reaching out to him too, still trying to educate him, inform the future decisions he needs to take? And if so, is the house doing that too?

"I went back to work; isn't that all that needs to be said?" He hears her closer again, standing beside him; and as he moves on down the garden, senses her in lock-step. "Don't answer that, because it isn't. I'll tell you that for free. I spent — oh, I don't know how long — weeks thinking about Eloise, that workshop. I used it as a mirror before which I hauled all those pivot points in my artistic life to see how they measured up, brought them before me as if I was a judge whose sole responsibility was sentencing the guilty. When I tried to be Bohemian or a Pre-Raphaelite, 'guilty'; when I pretended I was an exponent of Cubism or Dada, 'guilty'; when I tried to be a 'realist' or someone given up to abstraction, 'guilty'. And in each of those moments — moments that were supposed to be significant and transformational, don't forget that — I could still remember what I'd painted, more or less. And what

I'd sold. Or not sold." She laughs ironically. "In fact I was surrounded by what I hadn't sold, and whenever I came back here, to this house, the evidence was staring me in the face. There was no escape."

"Like the big picture on the half-landing wall?"

"Even so."

There would have been times in his own career when he would have failed, yet Owen is unable to recognise those manifesting themselves in the same way. Yes, an audit may not have gone well, or a report's findings might have been challenged, but such incidents were just part of the job. Although he took pride in what he produced, he was never attached to his output in the same way Maddie had been to hers. How could he have been? If such 'failures' rankled with him they would linger in his mind just a little while; and perhaps that had been the extent of it. And now? Now he simply no longer cares. He could press 'delete' on any such memories — and then empty the 'bin' with impunity. Evidently Maddie could not. Even now.

"That must have been hard." It is an inadequate word, one in a plethora of such words whose use he fears will do Maddie scant justice or offer little help.

"Like being continually slapped around the face. Yet they were reminders of all the good things I'd done, too. You could put that spin on it if you wanted. And it *was* quite a portfolio. One to be proud of. But more than anything all the pictures hanging in the house, everywhere you looked, were primarily reminders of something else: of avenues that ended up mere cul-de-sacs; examples of me falling short; the proof of my limitations. The kind of limitations Eloise simply didn't have."

He waits a moment, then: "I'm sorry."

She laughs.

"What have you got to be sorry for?"

"I meant I'm sorry that you weren't able to find that one thing which would have — I don't know — made it all worthwhile." Was that what he meant? "And I'm sorry that I didn't understand better. Or that I didn't help more..."

Feeling a strange chill, he shivers.

"I know," she says. "Thanks."

XVII

"Did you ever paint the garden?" Owen is standing beyond the apple trees, left foot gently tapping against a plank on one of the raised beds, a plank which has managed to free itself from the nails that once held the end nearest him in place. It is now bent outwards, warped slightly by seasons of rain, as if seeking complete release from its bonds and make good its escape across the lawn. He glances to the other end of the bed where it remains fixed. "Didn't you say you painted views from your bedroom window? But I can't recall anything from out here, or" — he twists slightly — "looking back up to the house."

He shivers again as the sun darts behind a small cloud. In the sky he notices a grey mass in the distance, approaching the town. George would have known such a cloud's portent and, if rain, how long it was likely to take to get here.

"Of course I did."

Owen notes a sense of dismissiveness in Maddie's voice, yet it is a tone which seems filled more with assumption than certainty.

"Sketches for sure." She rows back a little. "Mainly from up on the patio, sitting on the bench, facing one way or another. I think I remember something with the arch in it."

He allows a brief gap before: "And?"

"And nothing. Not really my thing."

"You never tried landscapes?" Owen thinks of the sketch of the beach now resting back on the bench and realises how daft his question is.

"Not in the sense you probably mean. I was never going to be another Constable was I? And anyway, rather than paint flowers where they grew I'd much prefer to put them in a vase juxtaposed against something obscure. Or contrary. For me there was more interest in tension, less so in beauty."

To Owen her answer feels a little too 'pat', a pre-prepared platitude ready to be dished out to anyone who had proven themselves sufficiently ignorant to ask the question in the first place.

"If you were to go through my sketch books I dare say you'd find the odd thing or two — a bit like that beach scene — but never anything more substantial than that. Not really. I don't think they appealed, gardens and such like. And anyway, I didn't need to capture this place did I? It was ours, here for us; it didn't need interpreting."

"Is that what you did, interpret things?"

"You might say that. Some people talk about getting to the 'truth' beneath the skin of something, and that notion may have some validity; but this house never needed unpeeling like that. Or rather, I never felt the need to go searching for something hidden under its skin; it was just fine as it was."

Owen contemplates the large brick building standing solid at the top of the garden. He too had never questioned it. It had always been there, reliable, immutable, behind every door a different realm — and one of them his own. And until this afternoon he had remembered it as a house filled with nothing but their truths. Perhaps that was one of the reasons it seemed such a stalwart in their lives, because of its constancy, because it never traded in falsehoods. Or never seemed to.

Yet now he finds himself knowing that premise is not as cast-iron as he had always believed it to be. He recalls again the conversations with Florence — her confession about Augustus' first engagement and her own childhood sweetheart — and feels that his faith in the place has been slightly shaken. Secrets lurked everywhere it seemed, even in Alma Road. Indeed, hadn't his pulling of the key from his coat pocket been one such deception — though of himself or of Maddie he isn't sure. And in unlocking the front door, had he perhaps unlocked more than just memories and time? Was truth — like that board in the raised bed — also trying to make a run for it?

"Do you remember that conversation with Florence about uncle's military ambitions?"

With Maddie's question as a trigger, Owen returns to his aunt's narration of George's family history and tries to find a related thread.

"What made you think of that?"

"There in the veg patch, the trace of a trench, which I assume would have been for potatoes or carrots or something."

He scans the surface of the bed, attempting to filter out the mass of weeds to see if doing so will reveal the undulations in the soil beneath. There is indeed a trench of sorts, shallow and short, but there nonetheless.

"Trench equals war? In a suburban back garden in England?" He smiles. "Marginally tenuous, don't you think?"

But it is more than that. As he looks up, as if resurrected at Maddie's whim, he sees Florence in her gardening attire, trug in hand, leaning on a fork.

"Did you know that your uncle nearly went to fight in the Korean war?"

She had delivered her question to them as if it were an irrelevance, the kind of inconsequential thing one let slip after a third glass of wine.

"Korea?" Maddie had looked up from where she was bent over the border examining the structure of a rose's petals.

Florence glanced her way, seemingly surprised that anyone would be bothered to expand her question into a fully-fledged conversation. Briefly looking back at Owen, she then lifted the fork and began turning the soil again.

"Korea, yes." A slight hiatus as she shifted some earth. "I suppose it was a hang-over from the war, all that nonsense about him 'doing his bit'." Another lift and turn. "He was old enough to make his own decisions by then of course, and the Second World War was still just about a recent memory."

"What stopped him?"

Florence looked at Owen as if he had fallen into an obvious trap and posed the wrong question.

"His family, I suppose. And perhaps he saw sense."

"You had nothing to do with it?" Maddie asked.

"How could I?" Florence transferred her tone of mild frustration onto Maddie. "I was still a teenager and didn't meet him until about five years after it finished."

"But he told you?"

Re-thrusting the fork into the ground, Florence walked over to Maddie and handed her the trug.

"You might as well cut some of those for the house."

For a few moments Owen and Florence watched as Maddie snipped blooms from the bush, the snap-snap of the secateurs accompanied by birdsong and the odd car passing nearby.

"Yes, he told me. Of course he did." Florence returns to her narrative without taking her eyes from Maddie. "But not until much later, until we'd been married for some time in fact. It wasn't something he'd previously felt he could speak of — especially as he didn't go. It would be, I don't know, like boasting about being an astronaut because one day you thought you might be even though you never were."

Owen laughed. "I can't see uncle in fatigues peeling potatoes in the mess hall."

"Or on his front in a jungle somewhere taking pot-shots at a bunch of other people laying down on their bellies."

"You can laugh," Florence admonishes them, "but he was serious about it for a while — and, for a much longer while than that, torn that he hadn't gone. Family tradition perhaps. It wasn't the kind of thing you got over in a heartbeat. Nor extinguished with a few jokes."

"I didn't mean..." Maddie stood up, about a dozen roses in the bottom of the basket.

"I know you didn't, dear. And in the end he did get over it, that's all that matters. I think for a while your uncle struggled with this bizarre blend of guilt and duty, honour and — I don't know what else. Something else. It was good that he didn't go, of course. For all of us."

Owen looks to where the rose bush has become unruly thanks to a lack of pruning, and is certain that its flowers will have been be nowhere near as abundant or perfect as they had that day. Were he compiling a list, the roses would be something else to add to it, another component requiring attention like the hedges, the vegetable patch, the picture rails, the stair carpet. Love of the place prevents him from wanting it to be a long and intimidating list. He hopes not.

"In some respects" — they were back in the kitchen now, Florence busying herself at the kettle, Maddie filling a vase with water — "your uncle was a little bit like Augustus in that regard."

"How so?" Owen, having lost the thread of his aunt's thoughts between vegetable patch and kitchen, needed reorienting.

"Having a particular notion of what being a man or husband meant, as if there was a template for such a thing." She pulled a tea caddy from a shelf and put two bags into a pot. "Maybe that was another hang-over from the war. Men went to fight, men protected things: land, women, children. Men earned the bread, and then defended it once they had it."

"Surely Augustus never wanted to fight?" Having filled the vase, Maddie put it on the counter beside the sink and started filling it with flowers from the trug.

"No, of course not." Florence allowed herself a short laugh. "But he possessed some traits from that superficial 'manliness' without doubt. And later — once he'd started to get the hang of things with you two — there were parts of the 'father and husband' template that started to appeal to him. Or he thought appealed to him."

Owen noticed the qualification.

"You sound like you're not sure."

"That he might have been just playing the game?" Florence considered her brother's attitude for a moment. "Alice wouldn't have been much different. They were still so young really — in terms of maturity as well as age — just trying to piece their lives together. I'm sure they watched their friends, Augustus his work colleagues, and tried to pull together a photofit of what they thought they should aspire to based on the components of others' lives that seemed the most attractive."

"Isn't that what we all do?" Maddie moved to the kitchen table and placed the vase at its centre, standing back a moment to admire her handiwork before returning to the sink to tidy up.

"I suppose so." There was an air of defeat in Florence's voice, one she was unable to refrain from showing. "How else are we to learn? But what I can't understand — then and now — is why people insist on giving labels to themselves. You're a 'this' or a 'that', a one thing or the other. There seems so little flexibility. Why can't people be what and who they are and leave it at that? It seems we're always seeking approval or qualification, recognition or measurement against a standard of some sort. God knows, we're far more complex that a simple label." A frown crossed her face as she stirred the tea pot and then set it alongside the flowers. "Very nice, dear."

To the best of his recollection, Florence had never labelled either of them. First and foremost, she preferred to assign attributes and abilities. Owen wonders if that was why it had been so important to her that Maddie had been brilliant. Perhaps she thought that being called an 'artist' was fundamentally meaningless. As he looks down at the remnants of the trench, Owen wonders how she might have labelled him had she been forced to do so. He can rule out 'husband', because he never was one; and there were a few things to which he might once have aspired (the equivalent of Florence's 'astronaut'?) that are similarly redundant. Indeed, how might he have labelled himself? Until a few weeks ago 'auditor' was the obvious option; but that was to allow oneself to be defined by what you did. Surely it didn't represent who he was as a person. And if it did, more shame on him.

It is a conundrum which defeats him, and so he chooses to turn and head back towards the house.

"I chased labels, Glen; you recognise that?"

"Did you? I always had you pegged as 'sister', 'artist' and 'brilliant'; I didn't think you needed any others." He thinks for a moment. "I don't think any of us did."

"It happened partly because of the circles in which I moved." Maddie ignores her brother's compliment. "When people met you they wanted to know what you 'did'. To say you were a painter or a sculptor wasn't granular enough; you had to be 'attached' to a movement, a style, a genre. You either painted portraits or you didn't; you liked abstraction or you didn't. Remember what I said about binary decisions? And of the things I chased — styles of living, of representation, of *being* almost — in a way none of those were for me. On one level I was doing all that chasing in order to meet other people's expectations, so that I could be defined by them. If you told someone you did a bit of everything they would scoff and assume that you weren't serious. Serious people knew who they were, what they were doing, had firmly nailed their colours to some mast or other." She pauses. "Does that make sense?"

"I thought you said you were trying to find your artistic home, the place you could fulfil yourself."

"I did. But maybe it was the other thing too. On reflection, maybe it always was. We all need to be accepted, don't we?"

Knowing how hard he had wanted Grace or Lisa or Wendy to accept him, it is an argument to which he can all too readily subscribe. Looking up at the house he knows there was never any issue with acceptance here; Alma Road and the people who lived in it never demanded anything of him, not really.

But what of now? If he is no longer an 'auditor', what does that make him? At the moment he is simply a man walking the garden of a house he currently owns and soon will not. Is there a word for that? And beyond the hedges, the rusted gate, what is he to the outside world? Unemployed perhaps, or 'between jobs'. Or is he 'retired'? Is that how he will be seen? Maybe he is to be pitied? Or celebrated? No, celebration would be going too far. If someone were to stop him in the street and ask "What are you?" what would he say?

"It's an important question, don't you think?" Maddie's voice comes to him softly from somewhere over his left shoulder.

He imagines her just a step or two behind him, instinctively bending her head to avoid the low branches of the apple trees.

"After all," she continues, "you're the only one left for whom the question is valid."

"Does that make me 'alone'? Is that a word I should be using?"

"If you think it fits — though it plainly isn't enough on its own, is it? You're more than that."

He can think of nothing profound. He is 'comfortably off', without 'economic pressures'; he is 'his own man', free to do as he chooses. Yet perhaps it is this last which is the cause for greatest concern — not simply because what such freedom means is as yet undefined, but also because it demands of him a decision.

"I envy your knowing what it was you always wanted to do." It is an observation logically arising from his own fog.

"Even if I failed?"

"If you think that fits…" His echoing of her own words forces Maddie to laugh. "But — for what it's worth — you were never a failure in our eyes. Whereas in my case…"

"In your case?"

"I was never a success." Owen leaves the word there for a moment, imagines it as if it were a windfall apple rotting on the lawn, ready to be crushed underfoot. "And now I'm in limbo, ready to take my next step but not knowing what it should be. The past is clear enough — isn't it always? — but the future… I simply don't know."

He wished they were with him now, Florence and George; wishes he could seek their counsel.

"Have you thought about what you *don't* want to do?" Maddie asks. "Or how you *don't* want to be labelled. You could always approach your dilemma from that angle, from the other way round."

"And that works?"

Florence had known what she didn't want, how she didn't want to be labelled. As soon as she found that she was 'a wife', the prospect of also becoming 'a mother' terrified her.

"Once upon a time," she had begun, an odd enough beginning made even more unusual by the fact that she and Owen had been in the memorial garden laying flowers — roses — at Maddie's stone. It was the first anniversary of her death. "I hadn't wanted children." She sensed Owen turning to look her way. "Oh, I know it's a strange enough thing to confess after all this time, especially as we're standing here, you and I. And Maddie…" Owen placed a hand on her arm, yet immediately sensed it was not comfort his aunt was seeking. "But I had children after all, in spite of what I wanted. Or thought I wanted." She sighed and edged them away and back to the path. "And I'm grateful for the two of you, I really am. Grateful that you were able to show me how wrong and selfish I'd been. You lit up our lives, gave it meaning. I only wish…" Her voice trailed away.

"Yes?"

"I only wish I'd told Maddie — you know — before it was too late. Though whether it would have made a difference…"

"Even though she became increasingly fragile and dislocated, I think she knew."

"Do you? Thank you, dear." They walked a few paces. Although the trees were still largely in leaf, there was a jag in the air. "And your uncle was grateful too. Of course he would never have said anything remotely emotional even if he'd had the notion to."

"Not his style," Owen concurred with a smile. He looked up at the broken sky, allowed them to walk on a little further. "And uncle, did he want children?"

Florence's face softens.

"From the outset. Perhaps it was because he came from a large family and missed that, what with the war and all. Or maybe it was in his genes, how he was made up, I don't know. But something had put me off. Living with your father possibly." She tried a laugh as if she were checking a coat for size. It was an uncomfortable fit. "So, as far as wanting children was concerned, he did and I didn't. We talked about it a lot. And then I found out I wasn't able to have children."

Stopping by the entrance gates, Florence walked slightly to one side and made for a nearby bench.

"Do you mind if we sit?" she asked.

Owen, assuming she had been overcome with the visit and wanted to compose herself, immediately sat alongside.

"Except I was," she said abruptly, her words like the soft 'pop' of a cork.

"You were what?"

"Able to have children." She paused for a moment. "There was nothing wrong with me. I could have had children if I'd wanted. I knew that and yet I told your uncle otherwise."

It seemed such a fundamental lie — and one totally at odds with how he knew his aunt to be — that Owen needed a moment or two for it to sink in.

"But why?"

She shrugged — a gesture which was also incongruous.

"Fear, I suppose. Wanting to protect myself and the life I wanted for your uncle and I; the one I'd mapped out."

"But isn't that understandable?"

"Perhaps. But it was still dishonest."

They were interrupted by the crunch of footfall on the path as a flower-laden couple passed them on their journey from the entrance into the depths of the garden. Owen nodded respectfully.

"I was working at the hospital then," Florence resumed, watching the walkers. "You may not remember I suppose; I gave up full-time nursing when you came along." Owen shakes his head. "It was a time of great advances in all sorts of areas, medicine included. The contraceptive pill came out in the early sixties. There were trials; our hospital was in one of the areas chosen. I volunteered."

"To be a guinea pig?"

"Don't sound so surprised, dear. It was perfectly safe by then, its efficacy proven to many decimal places. Given where George and I were in terms of the children debate — and given my preference — it seemed the logical thing to do. So I went on the trial. It was fine. And I never came off them, not until years later when I knew it was safe to do so." She allows Owen a moment to join the biological dots. "And in any case, we'd inherited you and Maddie by then, so in a way George's wish had come true."

"What did he say?"

"George?"

"Yes. About the pill."

Florence fiddled with the bottom button on her coat for just a moment.

"I never told him. As far as he was concerned I simply couldn't have children. He accepted my assertion at face value. Then, six years later, along you and Maddie came and it didn't seem to matter any more." She stands.

From where he remained sitting, Owen said "Do you wish you had?"

"Told him?" She smiled, waited for him to stand. "It would have broken his heart. And probably mine too." She moves off. "There are lies and lies, don't you think? White lies and grey lies and dirty black ones. I always hoped mine was at the lighter end of the spectrum — but please don't tell me what you think. Let's just leave it at that, shall we?"

XVIII

Owen reaches the patio before Maddie next speaks. Turning as if she is just behind him, he cannot fail to notice how the sun has sunk even lower, the shadows grown a little longer. There is nowhere else he needs to be, but he knows he will leave soon.

"You would never have known," she says.

"Known what?"

"That they had that between them."

"Florence's secret?" Owen imagines acknowledgement from his sister. "But it wasn't between them, was it? As a real secret it simply wouldn't have got in the way, at least not from uncle's perspective."

"Do you think he guessed?"

How could Owen possibly know? Their uncle had been quiet, unassuming, limiting emotional demonstration to topics about which he felt he could be intellectually expansive: injustice, the environment, ancient history. And the private topics? Owen is unable to recall any incident which may have suggested discord between him and Florence; no raised voices after they had gone to bed, no gesticulating at the bottom of the garden when he and Maddie were out of earshot. There had been harmony — even if he suspected it was harmony on his aunt's terms.

And yet George was far from stupid or unobservant. Might he not have noticed a packet of pills mistakenly left out one morning and then asked his wife what they were for? Or if not that, simply read the label on the box? Had Florence succeeded in being that careful, that discreet, and for such a long time? "It would have broken his heart" she had said, and if that were indeed the price potentially to be paid for the risk she was running, might she not have been indescribably vigilant, protecting her secret as jealously and as totally as she had protected the two of them? If subterfuge resided anywhere then surely it was only on her side.

"I don't know,: Owen says. "I want to say that I doubt it, for both their sakes — but how can you be sure about something like that?"

"There are things you know, things you *think* you know, and things you don't. Isn't that right? Isn't that how we navigate through life?"

"Along with all your binary decision points you mean?"

"When you boil it all down, is there anything else?"

Owen sits on the bench once again, glancing at his watch. Just a few more minutes. Yet he knows Maddie isn't finished with him yet — and he suspects the house isn't either.

"A somewhat nihilistic vision, don't you think? What about love, emotion, belief?"

Maddie laughs at her brother's naïvety. Owen senses her somehow encircling him.

"That's very noble coming from you, Glen."

He ignores her gentle barb.

"Just based on my experience, that's all. And the choices we make, the decisions we take."

"But whatever you may say, aren't they still all binary? And isn't love and hate and all that stuff also based on what you do or do not know, and how you respond to that? If I don't believe in war or if I fear nuclear destruction I may, in consequence, decide to support nuclear disarmament. And how much I support such a cause will drive my actions: I will or will not write to my MP, go on this or that march, take direct action." Owen says nothing, but Maddie can tell he is thinking. "What?"

"I don't know," he says, his stalling almost immediately proving Maddie's point, "I think I always assumed you were less — dogmatic. Being an artist and all. I thought you were supposed to embrace ambiguity, the essence of things, their non-black-and-whiteness."

"Yes, in theory you're right. But only to a point. Only to the point where the veil is drawn back, when something you didn't know suddenly becomes something you did. Or if not known, then realised, or seen... And in the realisation or the vision, you face the danger of having to deal with it."

At the end of the garden, a squirrel scampering across the vegetable patch distracts him for a moment; then her voice brings him back.

"And that includes you."

"Me?"

"Because whether you realise it or not — indeed, whether you like it or not — you see, know, realise things that you didn't when you walked through the front gate about an hour ago. And all that knowledge changes what you will do, the choices you will make."

"About what?"

"What next. Remember?"

More echo than flashback, Owen recalls their earlier exchange. He was sure the he or she had been the source of the original question — "what next?" — though it seems undeniable that any initial answers offered would certainly have been Maddie's. The house had formed at least part of her gambit, provided the framework for her argument. He had batted related notions away, but an hour had passed and — in accordance with her theory — he now recognised things he hadn't known before. And he can only concur with her in that new knowledge changes the questions we ask of ourselves.

"It does — and all the time," Maddie says, intruding on his thoughts once more. "How can it not? The questions shift, become more or less relevant, more or less redundant."

"You believe that?"

"I know it." A pause, before she quotes back to him: "'My experience'. What else is there?"

Owen wants to protest. He wants to object to her position by pointing out all the other factors that define what each of them did — and, in his case alone, might still do. There are platitudes he could trot out, like "no man is an island", yet he suspects Maddie will be able to swipe these away with consummate ease, knowing she is untouchable, finally freed beyond the mundanity of it all.

"That workshop," she begins again.

"Eloise," he says, proving once again that he has been paying attention.

"You asked me whether I carried on afterwards. Or how I carried on afterwards. And I did of course, but it was no more than me going through the motions. I had paintings that needed to be finished, submissions that needed to be finalised. My diary didn't suddenly empty because I had found myself undone by Eloise's genius. I still had a life to lead; obligations to be met I suppose. But those obligations weren't to myself as much as they were to other people, other things."

"Other people?"

"Those expecting me to show up, do something. And to Jimmy, who I was living with at the time; the Jimmy who never really understood what was going on, floating about in that innocent haze of his, a haze often embellished by weed or a little coke. He was the kind of character who tried to steer clear of the binary, who stupidly believed in the fluidity of things. How could I tell him what seeing Eloise had done to me?"

Owen senses his sister is reaching the crux of her story, the reason she has been following him around the house for the last sixty minutes. He had assumed her doing so had been for his benefit, but suddenly he is not so sure.

"Which was?" He resigns himself to the role of prompter.

"Drawn back the veil. Like I said. Demonstrated what I had feared all along, the knowledge that I'd been ducking for years, choosing to throw myself into new projects that were nothing more than artistic body swerves. And all just in case... Well, in case one of them turned up trumps. But seeing what Eloise could do and how easily she could do it made all that irrelevant. It was as if it had vanished in a puff of smoke."

"It?" Owen is conscious that Maddie has stopped moving, yet he is unable to identify the precise location of her voice.

"Everything, I suppose." In the small gap Maddie leaves, Owen sees the squirrel once again, hopping back into view from where it had disappeared. "My hopes and ambitions. Let's start there. Without realising it she had proven not only that there *was* a higher level which could be attained, but also that I had insufficient talent to get there — no matter how hard I tried, or what I tried. Don't get me wrong, I knew I was good — far from the worst at that workshop (you should have seen some of them!) — but simultaneously that I wasn't good enough. Not good enough to get where I wanted to be. Not good enough to be brilliant. Not good enough for me."

From wherever the word 'brilliant' has emerged, Owen imagines it slipping down the garden, dodging the apple trees, before disappearing over the vegetable patch into the bushes beyond. And he wonders whether it shouldn't be heading in the opposite direction, back into the house; after all, it was there it had been born, there the notion had been seeded, the evidence kept. He twists to look over his shoulder and up to the house, imagining himself back in Maddie's room.

But then again, perhaps it was right for the word to be off elsewhere, as if it were escaping, escaping from where it had been tethered to Maddie as much as she had been bound by it.

"And it wasn't just that realisation, Glen. I saw the past — my past — for what it was: a waste of time. Decades spent chasing an impossible dream; years of being egged on, encouraged, both here" — he imagines her pause is to look at the house as he has just done — "and elsewhere. Yes by people who were wanting the best for me, but by others too who simply didn't realise that in doing so they were tying the knots that bound me tighter to my fate."

From somewhere a road or two away Owen hears the toot of a horn and the squeal of breaks. There is a shout, and then peace is seemingly restored.

"Call it nihilism if you want to, but all I knew was that no matter how many more years I had, the number of wrong turns I took — or right ones, come to that — or the ever-increasing numbers of pills I took to keep me in the game, I could never be who I wanted to be. Never. Mine was an impossible quest. It had been from the start."

"Don't most of us start out with dreams that never get fulfilled? Me, George, Florence. Even our parents. Isn't that just the way things are?"

"'Shit happens' you mean?" She laughs softly and briefly. "I found myself looking back, reexamining my life and all those 'artistic moments' — if you can call them that. All the examples I could think of when I thought I'd done something good and worthwhile, those times I had garnered praise that meant something to me, when I had seemingly come so close… And one by one I was able to rub them out, negate them, disqualify them. And the harder I tried to salvage something from the wreckage of my life's work, the faster it all seemed to slip through my fingers. All that time, all that effort, all those broken dreams... increasingly chased down by uppers in the way an alcoholic chases beer with a scotch. Just one more never hurts, does it?"

Owen makes to stand, as if doing so would break the spell and free both he and Maddie from whatever has them in its grasp. But her words keep him pinned to the bench.

"And perhaps the worst thing of all? I might have been able to survive all that rubbing out of my past efforts if I could have imagined the future working out; if Eloise — consciously or unconsciously — had also been able to demonstrate what I needed to do to get where I wanted to be, even with my limited skill-set. But with the past went the future too. All I could see was more of the same: the same kind of painting, the same lurching from one style to another, the same rejections by galleries and competitions, the same dependencies. I had become blindly addicted to an unchanging horizon as far as I could see; flat, featureless, bleak."

"And was there no-one to help you navigate through all of that?" He takes a moment to clarify. "I don't mean me or Florence — sounds like we'd done enough damage — but, I don't know, wasn't there anyone?"

Snippets of Maddie's history come back to him like parts of stories recovered from the tattered pages of an ancient book of fables. A paragraph here, a paragraph there. And even though the titles of many of her stories bore the names of either an artistic movement or a man — like Jimmy (was he the last?) — Owen is aware that he knew none of those individual narratives from beginning to end. She had dropped hints, breadcrumbs — maybe even gingerbread crumbs — along the way, but as much as they may have proved to be an inadequate trail at the time, now they are even less efficacious, the words themselves worn away by the passage of time. Did he remember Jimmy, for example? Had he even met him? Names float before him and he is unsure whether they are relevant or not. As far as he can see, Maddie had no equivalent to his own more in-depth experience; no Grace, Lisa or Wendy upon which complete legends might have been built. Even flawed ones. Yes, his love-life had been no more successful than her own — even if operating on an entirely different plane — but at least his were narratives with a beginning, a middle, and an end. Indeed, all three women had walked this very garden, slept inside the house, made their mark on the place — however modest. But Jimmy and the rest? Hardly. To Owen such anonymous men seemed to be comprised of beginnings and endings alone. Or perhaps just endings.

If Maddie's relationships occupied a strange kind of fog for him, he wondered if a similar cloud hung over her, followed her around. He imagined it a cloud without substance; wave your hand and the mist would part, and you would be none the wiser in terms of what you had been looking at, or where it had gone. In the end the names made little difference. As far as Maddie was concerned, was 'Jimmy' and the rest nothing more than signifiers for something else?

"Failure," she suggests. "Each and every one. Did you realise I never went out with a guy who had the same name as any of my previous boyfriends? I don't think that was superstition, but I suppose you might see it that way… Each time I had seen into the hollow heart of my artistic endeavours, and when Jimmy and everyone else proved so totally incapable of helping me out of the mire, I came to see my 'love life' as some kind of bizarre parallel. Art imitating life. Or is it the other way round? They too were pointless, all these prior men; each one an attempt to find something, just like my lurching from one style to the next. If only Tracey Emin hadn't beaten me to it I might have come up with my own version of that tent thing of hers."

"But you might have been successful," Owen protests. "You might have found a man who one day *would* have saved you, given you what you wanted, made at least part of your dream come true."

"But that incarnation of me you're imagining was never a dream of mine, the 'happy ever after'. I never wanted to settle down and have kids, live in a house like this, mow the lawn on Sundays, join the local bridge club or whatever. Almost totally the opposite. Men were secondary really. I embarked on relationships in order to further my work; that's probably why I chose so many unsuitable — not to say unsavoury — characters. That's why Jimmy could never save me, nor any of the others; I hadn't picked them for that purpose. They were there to challenge, stimulate — even cause pain sometimes - in order to inspire me, to give me material for my art. Did I see that clearly at the time? Probably not. Did those failures have a cumulative negative effect on me? You've been made aware of my medical history. My medication history." She pauses for a moment. "I was a million miles away from what you wanted for me."

"Me?"

"When you talk about being 'successful', you're actually talking about having *your* version of the dream fulfilled, not mine; that one day you'd find a Grace-Lisa-Wendy who would serve up the destiny you wanted. And maybe even do so in this house. Work was something you did to pass the time, to fill up your bank account; it was never something you were passionate about. The complete opposite to me."

Owen thinks back, allows his eyes to wander both herbaceous borders. Dormant now, they would bountiful come next summer; bountiful and unruly, bountiful and different — in spite of their current similarities.

"Or the same," he suggests.

"In what way?"

"We were both crap at the thing that really mattered to us."

Maddie laughs. Despite knowing he has not expressed himself as well as he might have, the sound of her laughter forces him to smile. Perhaps it was just as well that he is clumsy with words. Sometimes, at least.

"What are we supposed to do now?"

Florence had been standing in Maddie's bedroom with her back to the window. Owen thought she looked lost. She seemed to scan the room as if it had suddenly been filled with foreign objects, items of no familiarity whatsoever. Following her gaze, Owen sensed a link had been severed, as if the entire contents of those four walls had been orphaned.

"I don't know," he said. "Presumably we need to decide what we want to keep and what not. Isn't that how these things work? Unlike you, I've never had to work through the belongings of a loved one."

"And so soon," Florence observed unnecessarily.

They had cremated Maddie two days previously and had just come in from the garden where they had scattered her ashes amongst the rose bushes. Although neither of them had said anything definitive, they both felt it was as good a place as any. At least it was within the compass of the house. If Florence had wanted to call it "coming home", she refrained from doing so. "Better here than somewhere nondescript in London" was all she would admit to.

After a short while she said "We'll keep the paintings obviously," then glancing to where various canvasses were propped against the wall, "we can sort through those later."

Owen imagined the two of them flicking through one canvas after the other, not really knowing what they were looking for.

"I'm sure we can find a home for the books," he suggested, "those we don't want to keep, I mean. And as for her clothes…"

"Hardly to my taste," Florence offered weakly. "Still, I daresay one of the charity shops in town will find them a good home."

Neither of them had moved. It was as if they had been locked in place by Maddie's departure, by the manner of it. Although walking through the bedroom door with the intention of sorting something out, resolving the unspoken, they had been paralysed in terms of both thought and motion. Owen knew that his aunt's question — "what are we supposed to do now?" — concerned more than mere goods and chattels. Perhaps it was closer to a plea than a question. Two years previously there had been four of them — geographically spread it had to be admitted, but four of them nonetheless. Three of them had been able to plan for George's departure, his illness always propelling him towards its inexorable conclusion, but in Maddie's case he and Florence had been caught off guard, defences down. She had taken them by surprise. The true subtext to Florence's question was "how are we to deal with what happened?"

When she verbalised this outright just a few moments later, Owen was prepared.

"Do you think we missed something?" she said, inevitably. "Do you think there was anything we could have done?"

"Don't think I haven't asked myself that same question," he said, "but how could we have known what was going on in London? Whenever we spoke to her she sounded upbeat, there seemed always something on the horizon to look forward to."

"But was there? Was there really? Or was that just a show she put on for us, knowing…"

"Well, if it was all a show" — Owen felt the need to protect his aunt — "then it was the same one she'd been performing for us for years."

"Owen!"

The admonishment served to highlight his clumsiness.

"I only meant that there seemed nothing different about her, that's all. Her rollercoaster lifestyle had been just that for so long, hadn't it? I suspect we may have spotted alarms when she was younger, but as we all got older — well, perhaps we became, I don't know, immune somehow. Perhaps there were never alarms. Or perhaps there were always alarms and she protected us from them. I don't think we ever realised the extent of her periods of depression, the medication she took."

"So you *do* think there was something we should have seen?" Florence was unable to keep a tone of desperation from her voice.

"I don't know, aunt."

And he hadn't known. In the previous few years they had all been experiencing difficulties: Florence with George; and even though a long enough period had passed, he was still trying to reconcile himself with the aftermath of Wendy. He tried to recall when he had seen Maddie for any extended period, or the last time he had spoken to her; and in examining every case he could find no clues, nothing upon which he could settle. And if he had, what then? He could only assume that this opacity was one shared with Florence; perhaps it had been worse for her.

A year later — almost to the day — they found themselves again in Maddie's old room. Owen had been visiting for the weekend and was leaving his own bedroom when he heard shuffling next door. Florence was sitting on the edge of the bed flicking through a collection of canvasses. The room itself was hardly changed, their efforts the prior year making little tangible difference on the fabric of the place.

"We never did sort through these," she said, looking up as soon as she realised he was standing on the threshold. "I thought I ought to have hung one or two, you know; and now it's probably time for me to decide which ones."

Owen moved to sit on the bed alongside her, noticing that she had yet to select any from the pile in front of her. He was reminded of George's jumpers.

"Any candidates?" he asked, as lightly as he could.

"Still making up my mind."

Florence pulled an abstract landscape from the pile and held it at arms length.

"I like this one, the colours especially; but I've no idea what it's supposed to be."

"Does it make any difference — if you like it that is?"

For a few minutes they sat rifling, Florence looking first, handing ones she most approved of to Owen for his judgement. It was a meditative if inconclusive process.

"You know, I'm surprised there was no-one from London who made any effort to get in touch, people who might have wanted a say." Florence broke the silence.

"A say in what? Did you think there might have been people who wanted to claim some of these?" Owen looked at the canvasses now resting in four piles, each of them having arrived at their current location indiscriminately rather than by scientific method.

"Why not? She had friends, people she worked with."

"Or lived with," Owen suggested.

"Precisely. What was the name of that last chap? Somewhat older than her if I remember correctly. Wasn't he an artist of some kind?"

"I don't think I ever knew much about him, if anything. Any anyway, from what Maddie said I got the impression that the people who were in her immediate circle were pretty much only interested in themselves. Seemed a bizarre kind of a life in many ways." He made a show of considering Florence's question further. "You know, I can't say I'm surprised that no-one was in touch. When did you last get the impression that Maddie was serious about anyone? I don't think she saw that much of a future in men; not really."

Florence passed him the last of the paintings, her action pretending decisiveness even if it lacked anything to suggest conclusion.

"I'm not sure about that you know," she said, having seemed to consider his assertion. "We women are made of different stuff. However much we protest about this or that, there are some things we can't escape — no matter how much we might want to."

And now, another five years further on, Florence's words come back to him afresh. Yet even though he has had all that time, all those months of hindsight in which to analyse and dissect them, Owen is still no closer to their deciphering. Perhaps under the pretence of talking about Maddie, Florence had been describing herself. Or then again, maybe she had travelled even further back in time to revisit Alice or unnamed others of her past acquaintance. Maddie had never shown any inclination to fall into step with convention, social or sexual. Surely she had made it her purpose — her quest almost — to do things her way; if there was a life to be led then she was going to live it in the way she wanted, not by anyone else's rules. And as it turned out, this had been her approach to death too.

"You know, even though I never wanted it, I came closer than you realise." Not quite a whisper, there is something subdued in Maddie's voice.

"Closer to what?" A late-afternoon breeze rustles the leaves of the apple trees.

"Your dream. The whole 'happy families' thing."

Trying to identify a man, a name, about whom he can recall her being even moderately serious, Owen draws a blank.

"I didn't realise there was ever anyone who was special. Certainly I can't ever recall you being 'enthusiastic'."

Maddie laughs again — but it is a laugh with no humour in it.

"I wasn't — and there wasn't — so your memory's not at fault."

"In that case I'm afraid you've lost me."

"How old was I?" Owen imagines her trying to remember. "I'd been in London just a few years, so probably mid-twenties. Twenty-five; nearly twenty-six. I suppose I was living the life I thought I should have been living; you know, the young artist at the edge of things, experimenting, exploring. I thought the world was my playground in those days, convinced that I could mould it to whatever shape I chose, wrap it about my little finger. It was one giant party. Those were the days when I was still idealistic."

It is a concept — idealism — to which Owen finds it hard to relate, almost as if he had been born with that element of his DNA missing. Had he ever been idealistic about anything? He likes to think he had, yet is unable to put his finger on precisely what the focus of that idealism would have been.

"I took — liberties. Thinking I owned the world in which I lived, that the ups and downs were all grist to my artistic mill. What was life for if not to provide me with my material?" A pause. "I was living with a guy called Roger. When I say 'living with', really we shared a flat, and — you know — occasionally a bed. It was a convenient arrangement, I suppose; almost commercial in some respects. No ties; no responsibilities. And then out of the blue I fell pregnant."

"Pregnant?" It is a word which, until that moment, he had unconsciously assumed never to have existed in Maddie's lexicon.

"Don't ask me how. Perhaps I'd lapsed with the pill; you know I was never very good at being methodical or rigorous. Or perhaps a condom had split. I don't know. But there it was, totally unexpected. Roger — not his real name by the way; I never knew that — immediately flew into a tailspin.

Like me, such a responsibility wasn't on his radar; it wasn't something either of us sought."

"You never said."

"No, I didn't. To be honest I'm not sure it ever occurred to me that I should. What was the point? It would only have served to set hares running. You know what aunt was like; she would have started to invent a whole new life for me. Maddie the artist *and* mother. If so, it would have been her picture, her template, not mine."

"Did you…" Owen is unsure how to phrase the next question.

"Think about keeping it? Yes, for a while. But not long. Not very long at all. Roger knew someone who knew someone… It was all arranged, quickly, silently. One weekend I was pregnant, the next I wasn't. Sometimes life can be that simple. Just another one of those binary choices, in its own way no more or less significant than any other."

Owen finds himself wondering how they would have coped, the rest of them; how the house might have accommodated a baby, even on an ad-hoc basis. And then he finds himself asking what if it had been Grace or Lisa or Wendy who had inadvertently become pregnant. What would that have done to them, to him? He wants to assume that at least one of them would have seen it through, changed the dynamic of their relationship, set out a new framework within which life could have been lived. His life. But it is, he knows, a somewhat desperate conjecture, certain the outcome would have been the same as in Maddie's case. Rejection.

"What happened to Roger?" As soon as he has spoken he knows it to be the wrong question, one he has asked because of the parallel he has drawn, placed himself in Roger's shoes. "I mean, how long did it take you to get over it?"

"Not long," Maddie says, ignoring his faut pas. "Or never. Take your pick. I confess I needed a little help to get me back on my feet."

"Help?"

"In the form of small round white pills that come in blister packs courtesy of an understanding female GP." She lets the message sink in. "Unsurprisingly I didn't stay in the flat much longer; it was Roger's you understand. As soon as I was able to leave, I had to. Oh, he didn't force me out; he was actually quite sweet about the whole thing. But once you've something like that between you…"

"And you never told us," he says again.

"What was the point?" Her answer is effectively the same. "It was over in a heartbeat — almost. The next time I saw any of you it was already in the past, calamity averted. Perhaps to myself I pretended that it had happened to someone else. And anyway, what's wrong with the odd secret here and there? We all have them, don't we? Don't you think this afternoon has demonstrated as much?"

Owen has a sudden desire to move, as if Maddie's confession is something which demands action — even after all this time. He stands and walks back toward the house, then begins another circuit around its perimeter. Nothing has changed other than the reach, shape and depth of shadow. Unsure whether he is relieved or hurt that Maddie chose not to share her trauma with him back then, he hopes this minor circumnavigation will either clear his head or provide some kind of clarity — and when he senses that she has chosen not to accompany him, he assumes that she is hoping so too.

When he reaches the front door Maddie is waiting.

"Do you forgive me, Glen?"

"For not saying?" He pushes against the door to ensure it is locked. "How can I not? I may not understand — and would probably have been even less likely to understand back then — but you're my sister and I love you. There's nothing to forgive."

On his way to the back garden, her voice accosts him just as he is about to duck through the archway in the hedge.

"I didn't mean about the baby."

Ahead of him the empty seat on the patio beckons; yet he has no wish to settle, suddenly discomforted, feeling off balance. He knows there is no need to prompt, to seek clarification, because something else is coming. To his left the three untended apple trees still stand heavily laden even though much of it has already fallen to the ground. He tries to recall what they tasted like, these apples, picked fresh from the tree, the journey between life and death over in an instant. Almost as a result of a whim.

"I thought I'd got over it of course," she is somewhere slightly ahead of him now, and Owen follows her as much as he is following her story. "The baby, I mean. I found a new place to live, reoriented myself, went back to work with new-found vigour. Perhaps that's what having a narrow escape does to you. Maybe that's how gratitude for a near miss manifests itself. Not that it actually made any difference. Not really. But I told myself that I had put it behind me; that I had moved on."

"But you hadn't?"

"The merry-go-round started again: new flat, new man, new paintings, same old story, same old pills. And although I couldn't see my life for what it was, I suppose I was happy enough; still flogging the same old dream, still deluding myself. Isn't there some saying about the definition of insanity?"

Though unable to settle on where he had come across it, Owen knew this one.

"Doing the same thing over and over again but always expecting a different outcome."

"Something like that. Until Eloise that is."

"When your world was really turned upside-down." He waits a moment. "But I still don't understand what it is you need to apologise for."

Not hearing an immediate response, Owen fears he has lost her; so he stops and listens, looking about the garden as if she might suddenly have been transformed into one of the wilting shrubs. But she is everywhere, of course.

"I don't think I'd thought about the baby in years; honestly I don't. But after that workshop later when I came to question the life I'd been leading and the dream I'd been chasing, the likelihood of being unable to get to where I wanted to be — no, the certainty of knowing I couldn't — then the baby came back to me. Like a ghost. Almost haunting me. As if it were saying 'look at what you could have had, the life you might have led, the person you might have been'. It was a realisation, a challenge which struck me hard. It had been unexpected, unwanted, and there it was telling me what else I'd lost, slapping me round the face, kicking me while I was down. And do you know what the worst part was?"

As if she were there to see him, Owen shakes his head.

"For the first time I truly wondered if I'd made a mistake, if I should have kept the child. But it was too late. I was nearly fifty and it was too late. It was all too late. I was a failure as an artist and I suddenly realised would never be fulfilled as a woman. I was on my own: a spinster with patchy portfolio at best and a track record of not very nice men-friends. When I looked around, all I could see was the detritus that made up my life. Even if there had been something left to cling to, I was suddenly too tired to do so."

It was the conversation Owen wished he had been able to have with her six years earlier, now realising that his lack of understanding had been yawning like a chasm before him ever since.

"I was a dab hand at taking pills by this point. So, one pill for each year — and one more for luck. It seemed appropriate, especially on the eve of my fiftieth birthday. After all, what was the point of going on? It was the last binary decision I ever made — and in some ways the easiest."

"We might have — I don't know — helped. Surely."

"Don't think I didn't think of you and aunt; but what could you have done? And how could I have carried on having been emptied out so comprehensively? Do you imagine I could have come back here, recolonised my old room, given up painting, got a job in Tesco or something?" She laughs ironically. "That version of my life would surely have killed me too — though more slowly and painfully. And for all the wrong reasons."

Having always felt betrayed by her suicide, Owen wonders how much more he understands now, how much closer he is to being able to decipher how she was, how she felt. That he is nearer he cannot deny, but is this new proximity sufficient? Is there any compensation to be had from it?

"There is for me."

Her voice, heavy with finality, comes from just above him now, between the trees and the house. It is a sound which forces him to turn and look at the impassive building standing guard over them. It had always been a benevolent force, and Owen has to believe that, had Maddie returned and enjoyed her fiftieth birthday with them, the house would have continued to do its best for her. Indeed, it might even have saved her.

And now, as he hangs his head, the inevitable question: what of him? Fifty-eight and unemployed, without any kind of passion to run from or to. Indeed, he remains what he feels he has always been, a superficial kind of a man lacking the imagination needed to comprehend all the things Maddie had done in her too brief life. And yes, even her suicide. Feeling as if he is finally saying a proper goodbye to his sister, he wonders whether, at that precise moment, there shouldn't be a another voice to accompany him. And then realises that it might have been there all along.

XIX

"I know we haven't been very successful in selling the house, but the market has been particularly difficult over the last few months." Stacey Wills flashes him her most professional smile then allows her eyes to glance back to the property details on the screen in front of her.

"The pandemic," he offers, "yes, I understand."

"But there are clear signs that the market is coming back." She hesitates. "Admittedly we haven't seen the kind of bounce-back some other towns and cities have experienced, but there have been more enquiries recently; our footfall is going up."

If Stacey is trying to be reassuring or persuasive, she is failing — and Owen thinks she knows it. In spite of his commercial background and his understanding as to what 'footfall' means, it is a word he has never liked and a concept he has never trusted.

"But not on Alma Road?"

"Indeed." She looks back to the screen. "We've asked ourselves if we might have got the pricing wrong when we made our proposal back in" — a pause to check — "late Autumn 2019 when you instructed us. On reflection it may have been a little 'punchy', but then we weren't to know that Covid was about to hit us. Having said that, the signs are there that the market is catching up. To reduce it now…"

"But as I said, I don't want to reduce it." Owen tries to be as definitive as he can without being harsh, watching her eyes to see of the prospect of lost commission is dawning more clearly. "And it's not a question of money. I simply no longer wish to sell it. I want to take it off the market."

"Actually I was hoping to line a viewing up this coming weekend."

Knowing what she wants him to say, he ignores her interjection, a last roll of the dice. "And for you to let me have all the keys back. That's all, Stacey. My circumstances have changed since I decided to sell the house. I understand there may be a small fee — but you've had long enough to move it on."

The agent smiles again, though a little more weakly, and reverts to consulting her screen. Owen wonders if that is where she is more comfortable, interacting with numbers, graphs, images and spreadsheets; whether she finds property easy and people hard. He can imagine her searching for a button on the display in front of her, the button she now needs to click in order to remove 17 Alma Road from her database. He leans forward slightly to see if he can make out what the screen might be displaying, but its angle is against him.

Her hand jerks on the mouse and the screen darkens.

"If you'll just give me a moment." And then she stands.

Two minutes later — having exchanged final pleasantries — Owen is back outside, his left hand manipulating the various keys now nestling in his coat pocket. Apart from the alien sensation of the tag the agency had applied to them, they feel somehow familiar, and he tries to identify the front door, back door, and garage keys by touch alone. Then, just as his fingers get to them, he remembers the additional two keys for the indoor rooms — George's old study (which he never knew to ever be locked) and the cupboard at the top of the stairs — and finally the smallest one of all for the garden shed's padlock. They are old friends, and soon they will be reunited with the twin sets of keys (one his, one Maddie's) which have been secreted at the back of his sock drawer since Florence died and he shut the place up.

Although he is nearing the end of his journey, it is as yet an incomplete one. What would make it whole? Being able to hand one of the sets of keys back to Maddie — and to find Florence and George reinstated the next time he walked through the front door. But Owen knows neither of those things are possible. In consequence, he feels strangely childlike again, orphaned once more and being thrown onto the mercy of someone else — though in this instance that someone else can only be himself.

Yet there is a constant. The house is there to welcome him, just as it had been some fifty-four years previously. It has outlived Florence and George and Maddie, just as it will him; but for now it will do, he and Alma Road against the world. And for a few strides as he walks away from the estate agent he is unaccountably thrilled again, perhaps just as he had been years earlier when running home with his 'O' or 'A' level results, or when he had opened the letter from Lancaster confirming his place at University. There have been other such moments peppered throughout his life of course; moments of joy, domestic or emotional. But on reflection it seems as if only a few of those were not tied to the house.

As he waits to cross the road at the lights — the shift from 'red man' to 'green man' suddenly symbolic — he wonders what else the house has in store for him, what else is left for them to share. Running ahead three weeks, he imagines the day when he will be steering the removal men between one room and the next, telling them where to leave chairs and tables, bags and boxes. And then the days that will follow as he unpacks and places, aligns and re-places, hangs and re-hangs; all the physical things in which their lives were encapsulated. And after that, when all the boxes are empty, collapsed and stacked, to sit in George's study — *his* study — perhaps sipping a glass of wine and wondering what comes next.

But that is to wish his life away.

Feeling lighter than he has in, oh, he doesn't know how long, he crosses the road and heads toward Alma Road again; his first task, to push wide that rusted old gate, insert the key in the heavy front door, and then begin to let the light and the life back in.

Milton Keynes UK
Ingram Content Group UK Ltd.
UKHW010724190224
438095UK00001B/29